Falling in Controlled Circumstances
By Pepper Espinoza

What would you dare for a free fall of desire and passion?

For four years, Gregory Jackson and his partner, Cambridge police chief Phillip Baker, have enjoyed a committed relationship. Neither suspect there's something missing in their lives. Until one fateful day when Phillip has a close call while on duty...and Gregory's flat tire puts him squarely in the glide path of dangerously charming American pilot Jim Tennant.

While Jim's in town to fly prototypes at the local air force base, Greg struggles to keep their relationship platonic, but Jim is an irresistible force. At the moment a transgression seems inevitable, Phillip surprises Gregory by encouraging him to take exactly what he wants. That night, all three of them really learn what it means to fly.

Gregory's pleasure is tempered by two serious concerns. Why is Jim interested in a relationship with a couple? And why is Phillip suddenly willing—even eager—to invite another man into their bed?

Warning: This title contains shameless flirting, playful banter, hot sex between two men, super-hot sex between three men, rule breaking and having fun.

Sins of the Past

By Amanda Young

Two men bonded by love. A long forgotten secret neither knew they shared in common.

Andrew Vought is a wealthy single parent who's all but given up on love. Ryan Ward is an up-and-coming landscape architect, who's never believed true love exists.

In each other's arms, they find the love they've sought. But can a budding new love survive the secrets both men harbor?

Warning, this title contains the following: explicit sex, graphic language and some hot nekkid manlove.

Falling Into Sin

A Samhain Publishing, Ltd. publication.

Samhain Publishing, Ltd.
577 Mulberry Street, Suite 1520
Macon, GA 31201
www.samhainpublishing.com

Falling Into Sin
Print ISBN: 978-1-60504-777-5
Falling in Controlled Circumstances
Copyright © 2010 by Pepper Espinoza
Sins of the Past Copyright © 2010 by Amanda Young

Editing by Sasha Knight
Cover by Scott Carpenter

Falling in Controlled Circumstances, ISBN 978-1-60504-262-6
First Samhain Publishing, Ltd. electronic publication: November 2008
Sins of the Past, ISBN 978-1-59998-599-2
First Samhain Publishing, Ltd. electronic publication: September 2007
First Samhain Publishing, Ltd. print publication: June 2010

Contents

Falling in Controlled Circumstances

Pepper Espinoza

Dedication

To Vivien, for the encouragement.

Chapter One

Gregory Jackson stared at the flat tire, with only one rather pointless question running through his mind. *How did this happen?* That seemed the most important question, because he certainly didn't have answers to any other possible inquiries. *Should I call Phillip?* He thought not. *How do I fix this?* He had no clue. *How far away is home?* Too far to carry all of his books, and he was not about to leave them. They weren't technically his to leave lying around on the side of the road.

He circled the car once. All of the other tires seemed to be in proper working order. He opened the boot and rummaged around. He appeared to have the spare and the tools necessary to swap out the flat for the new tire, but that actually didn't help him.

Call Phillip, his reasonable side urged. *If he gets home before you do, he'll worry. Plus, he's a cop. He'll know what to do.*

Gregory fished his phone out of his pocket, prepared to listen to the voice of reason, but his phone was off. Frowning, he tried to turn it on, but the lights didn't even flash. *Dead battery.*

"Oh...bollocks!"

"Bollocks? Is that British for *fuck*?" an American voice drawled from behind him.

Gregory spun around, his response dying on his lips. The stranger might have been an inch or two shorter than him, but he seemed bigger somehow. He wore an amused grin that lit his hazel eyes, and sunlight glinted off his golden hair.

"Uh...no, in fact. It's British for balls."

"Still not a very polite word."

"No, it's not."

"I didn't think people talked like that here in Cambridge."

"They do."

"What have you got? A flat tire?" the stranger asked, approaching the car.

"And a dead phone."

"Do you have a spare?" He didn't wait for an answer. He circled to the boot and peered inside. "And tools. Good. I guess you don't know how to change a tire?"

"No. I never had the chance to learn."

"Well, you do now. Come here."

It didn't occur to Gregory to question the command. "You don't have to go to any trouble. If you have a cell phone, I can just call my...Phillip."

"Nope. No phone. Besides, what kind of person would I be if I left somebody as cute as you stranded on the side of the road?"

Gregory wasn't sure how to respond to that. Did the stranger mean that as a genuine question?

"Well. I appreciate your help."

"I'm not helping out of the kindness of my heart, you know."

Alarmed, Greg took a step back and nearly stepped into the road, but the stranger caught his shirt and pulled him out of the way of oncoming traffic. "I'm in a relationship."

The smile never left the other man's face. "Good for you. But I think teaching you how to change a tire should at least be worth a pint. Don't you?"

Gregory felt the blush crawl up his neck. "Oh, of course. A pint. There's a pub I like not too far from here."

"Good. My name is Jim, by the way."

Gregory took his extended hand. It was warm, his fingers strong, his skin a little rough. He shook with a confidence that bordered on arrogance. How somebody could have an arrogant handshake, Gregory didn't know, but this Jim certainly did. Though it wasn't unpleasant.

"Gregory."

"Good to meet you, Gregory. Now get this jack, and I'll show you what you need to do."

Gregory might not have been a dab hand when it came to cars, but he was a quick learner when he set his mind to something. And it helped that Jim commanded his attention. Gregory couldn't have looked away, even if he wanted to. Jim explained each step of the process with ease, like he had taught Brits all over the island exactly how to change a tire. He never lost his easy, amused smile. Even when Greg made a mistake.

"No, you need to turn the bolts the other way. The other way."

Gregory grimaced. "I think I'm missing this part of my genetic code."

"There's a tire-changing part in the genetic code?"

"There must be." Gregory bit his lip and shifted direction, screwing in the bolt. "How did you get so good at this?"

"A lot of practice. I worked in the pit for most of my misspent youth."

"The pit of what?"

Jim laughed. "The pit crew. For car racing. You do have races here, right?"

"Yes. I think so."

"But you do know what I'm talking about?" The question wasn't unkind. In fact, Gregory wondered if Jim had an unkind bone in his body.

"Yes. So, I guess you could have changed this in..." Gregory checked his watch. "Faster than thirty minutes."

"Of course. But you wouldn't have learned then, right? I'm not always going to be around in the case of a flat."

"I appreciate your generosity. I mean it, really. This has been... You're a lifesaver."

His hazel eyes positively sparkled. "I guess I am pretty great. But I did have strong motivation. That pint, remember?"

"I think I owe you more than one."

Jim tossed the flat tire into the boot, then began gathering the tools. "I guess two will cover it. Unless you also want to join me for dinner."

"Dinner?" Gregory checked his watch and swore softly. "I might have to take a rain check on the pub."

"That's not very sporting of you."

"I know, but if I'm out, Phillip will worry and..."

Jim slammed the top closed and wiped his hands on his pants. The gesture drew Gregory's gaze down, and he noticed how well those jeans fit Jim's body. He was deceptively slim, but Gregory suspected he'd hold his own in most fights.

"Even if you're out repaying the man who saved you from untold catastrophe on the side of a busy road?"

"Probably."

"What if he joins us? Is he the sort of guy who enjoys a nice night at the pub?"

No. Gregory left that unspoken. Clearly, it was a rhetorical question. What sort of hard-working man didn't enjoy knocking back a few with his mates? Phillip didn't really have any mates. He didn't need them. He barely conceded that he needed a lover. But Gregory didn't think it would be impossible to convince him to go out for at least one drink.

"Do you have your car around here?"

"Nope. I don't drive. It still confuses me too much to be on the wrong side of the road."

"Well, thank you for abstaining from driving then. I wish more people would."

Jim laughed. "You have a hard time with Americans around here?"

"Not Americans, specifically. Incompetent idiots in general." Gregory colored. "Not that I think Americans are incompetent idiots. Not that I think you are, either. I meant that..."

"I know what you meant."

Jim pulled the passenger door open and settled in the front seat, leaving Gregory no other choice than to get behind the wheel.

"I actually don't know too many Americans," Gregory admitted as he started the engine.

"Really? You never hopped across the pond?"

"No. I've always wanted to visit America, though."

"Which part?"

"The Library of Congress."

Jim laughed again. "You aren't serious."

"I'm dead serious. I want to do a tour of libraries around

the world. I'm saving money now, but that sort of trip isn't easy to save for on my salary." At Jim's perplexed look, Gregory smiled. "I'm a librarian. At the university."

"Oh. I guess that would explain it, then. That would also explain all the books in the backseat too."

"Yes. So...do you still work in the pit?"

"Nah. I'm a pilot."

"You mean for airlines?"

"I test new planes and prototypes. I go all over the world. That's why I'm visiting this fair land. I'm working at Mildenhall."

"The air force base?"

"Yes."

Gregory swallowed. "Isn't that dangerous work?"

"It can be, I suppose."

"That doesn't bother you?"

"Not a bit."

Gregory wanted to ask more questions about that. He wanted to pick Jim's brain until he understood the other man. He had a nearly crippling fear of flying, and even if he managed to save his money for the trip around the world he always dreamed of, he knew he would never be able to do it. The thought of being in a plane made him sweaty and itchy. It made his stomach crawl up his throat.

"Would it bother you?" Jim asked.

"Honestly? I'd be too paralyzed with fear to even consider it."

"It'll take an awfully long time to cross the ocean by steamer."

"That has definitely occurred to me before."

"You should go flying with me some time."

Gregory stole a glance at him from the corner of his eye. "What?"

"You should go flying with me some time."

"I heard you the first time. I wasn't quite sure what you meant."

"I think it's a pretty self-explanatory statement."

Gregory nodded. "True enough. Okay, why should I go flying with you some time?"

"Because then you'll forget all about being afraid. That's the best way to overcome fears, you know. Face them head on."

"I'll think about it," Gregory promised.

"No, you won't."

Gregory blinked. "What?"

"You won't think about it. You're just saying that because you think you'll never see me again, and it's easier to end the conversation with a promise. Appease the madman who doesn't have the sense not to plummet to the earth at controlled speeds."

Gregory pulled to a stop and studied Jim's face. Was Jim having him on? Was he genuinely offended or upset? Was it a third option that hadn't even occurred to him?

"What do you mean about that last bit?"

"What last bit?"

"Plummeting to the earth at controlled speeds?"

"That's all flying really is. Falling in controlled circumstances."

"This doesn't make me want to get in an airplane, with you, or anybody."

Jim flashed him a smile. It was more than a smile. It was like Jim was gifting him with confidence, like he had so much he could afford to spare some. "I'm very good at controlling the circumstances."

"Somehow, I don't doubt that." Gregory guided the car down the narrow street and stopped outside a neat two-up, two-down. Phillip's car was already parked in its normal place. "Here we are."

"This is your house? It's nice. Is this your garden?"

"Garden? Oh, the flowerbed? Phillip has a green thumb. He says the flowers help him relax."

"Flowers are relaxing? I guess I never thought about them that way."

"It's not the flowers." Gregory smiled and pushed his door open. "It's the process. Not that the plants aren't beautiful, but he'd be as happy, I think, if they never bloomed at all."

"Flowers." Jim shook his head as he crawled out of the car. "I like that."

Gregory liked it too. Every Sunday morning, Phillip would dress in his jeans and a T-shirt, he'd bring Gregory out to the garden with him, and they would play in the dirt. Phillip always seemed to grow younger. It transported him, somehow.

Phillip was waiting for him at the door, wearing a heavy frown. "Where have you been? I thought you were going to be home by four today. Who is this?"

"Phillip, this is Jim. Jim, Phillip Baker."

"Jim?"

"Jim..." Gregory looked over his shoulder.

"Tennant," Jim said, stepping forward and offering his hand. "It's a pleasure to meet you, Mr. Baker."

"Chief Inspector Baker."

"It's a pleasure to meet you, Chief Inspector Baker."

"Jim helped me change my tire."

Phillip shifted his attention to Gregory, concern creasing his face. "You had a flat tire? Why didn't you call me?"

"My phone was dead. But everything's fine now. I offered to buy Jim a pint, in return for his help. But I thought you might like to come with us."

Phillip's lips thinned, and Gregory knew what the answer was going to be before he said it. "I can't."

"Why not?"

"I just dropped home to change my clothes and have some tea. We're doing some undercover work tonight."

"Something dangerous?"

"Not too dangerous."

Gregory nodded. He knew he shouldn't feel disappointed. This wasn't the first time Phillip had to leave for the whole night. It wasn't even the first time that week. "Do you want me to stay around then?"

"No, go have your pint." Phillip slapped him on the back. "I was just going out the door."

"Call me tonight, if you can."

"I will."

Gregory waited for the customary goodbye kiss, but Phillip merely nodded and ducked around them.

"Not a kiss goodbye, huh?" Jim asked once Phillip was out of sight.

Gregory glanced over. "Phillip isn't a big fan of public displays."

"This is public?"

"Public enough, I suppose."

"Seems like he was a bit ashamed."

Gregory stiffened. "What makes you think you have the right to say anything like that? You don't know anything about Phillip."

Jim held up his hands. "You're right. I'm sorry. That was out of line. In fact, I'll understand if you don't want to buy me that pint."

Gregory heard Phillip's car fire up and then disappear down the street. The night was going to be very long. Sometimes, Phillip didn't come home until after dawn. Gregory hated that—even if he should be accustomed to it by now.

"No. I want to go out. Come on. Pub's around the corner."

"How long have you two been living together?" Jim asked as Gregory locked the house.

"Almost two years now. We were together for two years before that."

"I guess I really was out of line. You sound like you have a solid relationship."

Gregory smiled. "Yeah, we do."

Jim shifted the topic of conversation as they walked, choosing instead to talk about how strange it was to be a Yank living in England. "I really didn't think it would be a big deal, you know? How different could things be here, after all."

"How different are things?"

Jim shook his head. "It's like a completely different world. I'm afraid if I get started on the difference, I'll never stop. But the worst thing is..." His voice faded, and he looked away.

"The worst thing is what?" Gregory prompted.

"Being alone."

"You're lonely?"

"You sound surprised."

"I am. A bit."

"Why?"

Because nobody as gorgeous as Jim Tennant could possibly be alone. Because nobody as gregarious as Jim Tennant should have a hard time finding somebody to talk to. Because Gregory was certain that as soon as they stepped into the pub, Jim Tennant would be surrounded. It wasn't his larger-than-life personality, but some other quality. Something Gregory couldn't quite put his finger on.

"It seems like you wouldn't have a hard time meeting people, is all."

"Oh, I've met people. I've met a number of people. But they aren't all worth my attention."

"How do you decide who is worth your attention?"

"It's easy enough. But I'm afraid if I tell you, you'll think I'm shallow."

"I won't."

Jim's gaze moved up and down Gregory's body, as slow as a caress. "The first consideration is a nice ass." He looked up and pointed to the building. "This the pub?"

Gregory blinked. "Yeah. Yeah it is."

"Great. I'm dying of thirst."

Gregory followed him out of the sunshine and into the pub's cool shadows. That was naked appreciation he'd seen in Jim's eyes. Which he could have ignored, if it hadn't accompanied shameless flirting. A sliver of guilt pierced him. Phillip was going out to clean the streets and keep the city safe from crime, and what was he doing? Flirting with a virtual stranger.

Though, Gregory supposed, he wasn't technically flirting with Jim. He hadn't responded to it, or returned the favor. As long as he continued to not return the favor, it would all be very harmless.

Gregory walked up to the bar. "Two lagers, please, Ralph."

"Sure thing."

"You come here often?"

"Yes. Well. We used to."

They settled at the table with their pints, and Gregory made it a point to keep a fair amount of space between them.

"Used to? What happened?"

"Phillip got his promotion. The youngest in his department to ever be promoted to chief inspector. But that means he doesn't have the spare time he used to."

Jim leaned forward, pinning Gregory with his sharp eyes. In the dim light, they seemed muted. But they were still arresting, still demanded attention. "Sounds like you're a bit lonely too."

"It's not too bad."

"How much time do you spend with him, on average?"

"What do you mean? In a week?"

"Sure."

Gregory stared down at the amber liquid. "A lot of time. I don't know how many hours. Several per day."

"I think you're lying."

"Why do you think you know so much?"

"Am I wrong?"

He sighed. "No. You're not wrong. But you do seem oddly interested in my personal life."

"You're right. I'm a naturally curious person. I get in a lot of trouble for sticking my nose where it doesn't belong."

"But you do it anyway." Gregory sipped from his beer.

"Why?"

"Fun, I guess. Don't you like to have a bit of fun, sometimes?"

"Not your brand of fun. You seem a bit out of control to me."

Jim smiled. His teeth were nice. Straight and white. The smile reached his eyes. Gregory wasn't sure how, but he was convinced that Jim did that on purpose—made his eyes light up, like twin stars in the night sky. "If it's only a bit, I must be doing something wrong. Tell me. What's it like to be a librarian?"

"I guess that depends on who you are. I think it's great. You'd probably be bored out of your mind."

"Maybe." Jim tilted his head back, and his Adam's apple bobbed as he took several deep swallows. The movement drew Gregory's attention to his throat. It was an oddly perfect throat. How could throats be perfect? The same way handshakes could be arrogant. "Why do you think it's great?"

"I clean and restore old volumes. It's like...I get to bring books back to life. Texts that may not have been seen or touched in decades, or even centuries." Gregory smiled self-consciously. "I'm not testing airplanes or anything like that, but..."

"Why do you do that?"

"What?"

"Don't put down your abilities. How many people in the world can do what you can? You're right. You get to bring books back to life."

Gregory's smile turned from self-conscious to pleased. "You really think that?"

"I wouldn't have said it otherwise."

Gregory eyed Jim's empty glass. "You made it through that quickly."

"I was thirsty."

"Want another round?"

"If you don't find my company objectionable."

"I don't. Yet."

"Then I'd love another round."

Gregory promised himself he'd stop after the second round. Certainly after the third. And then they'd part company and that would be the end of that. No harm, no foul.

Gregory blinked against the bright light, automatically covering his face with a pillow to block the glare.

"Oh. Sorry. I didn't know you were still awake. Or did I wake you?" Phillip asked, turning the light off.

"You didn't wake me. I've been waiting up."

"You know you shouldn't do that. You won't get any sleep then."

"And you know I can't sleep without you." Gregory rolled to his side and patted the mattress beside him. "Lay down."

"I can't."

"Why not?"

"I'm still dressed."

"Then get undressed, silly. Come on, I've missed you."

Greg watched as Phillip stripped from his work clothes. He didn't even bother to fold the clothes and set them aside. He left them in a pile in the middle of the floor. When he crawled into bed, he was trembling. Like he was cold. But it wasn't cold in the house—Gregory had kicked the blanket off the bed in frustration earlier that night.

"What's wrong?"

"Nothing."

He wrapped his arms around Phillip and pulled him close. The other man sighed and curled against Gregory's body, as though he was afraid somebody would try to pull them apart.

"What happened, Phil?"

"Somebody got hurt." His words were muffled against Gregory's shoulder, his breath hot.

"Who?"

"Somebody who was in the wrong place at the wrong time. She's at hospital now. They don't know if..."

Gregory stroked Phillip's short hair soothingly, his fingers curling in the soft strands. "It's not your fault, Phil."

"I was the officer in charge. It's my fault, by definition."

"No, it's not. You're not God. You can't see everything or know everything."

"I should have made sure the area was clear. I should have made sure nobody was there to get caught like that."

"What happened?"

"She was hit by the perp when he tried to make a getaway. He was so shocked when she went flying that he stopped, and we were able to get to the car before he sped off again."

"So, you got the guy you were after?"

Phillip nodded.

"That's good, right?"

Phillip nodded again.

"Do you want me to put on the kettle?"

"No. Just..." His arms tightened. "I want you to stay here."

"Okay."

Gradually, Phillip calmed, and the tremors beneath his skin subsided. Gregory concentrated on taking slow, even breaths, hoping that Phillip would unconsciously follow his example. The world saw Phillip Baker as a calm, assertive man. Always in control. Always without fear. The world needed to see him that way. But he was a normal human being too. He could be frightened. And angered. And shocked.

The first night Phillip had crawled into Gregory's bed without speaking, just shaking, Gregory had been freaked out. He didn't know what was wrong with his lover. He thought something horrific must have happened—like the death of a parent. After gentle coaxing and general comfort, Gregory had understood the truth. Sometimes, Phillip needed somebody to hold him, somebody he trusted.

"I'm sorry about earlier today," Phillip murmured.

"Why?"

"The way I left. I didn't even kiss you goodbye. I was..."

"You were wrapped up in the case. I know."

"That doesn't mean I have the right to be a jerk."

"You're never a jerk to me." Gregory brushed his lips across his forehead. "So don't worry about that."

"Did you have fun at the pub?"

"It was nice. Missed you, though."

Phillip's mouth was warm against Gregory's bare shoulder. "Tomorrow's Sunday, isn't it? We can go out in the evening."

"Why don't we have a nice lie-in tomorrow too? We can work in the garden in the afternoon."

"I like that."

"Good."

Phillip lifted his head and tried to pull away. Gregory refused to let him go, though. "Where do you think you're going?"

"I'm too wired to sleep. And I don't want to keep you up all night."

"I'll help you sleep."

Gregory heard the frown in Phillip's voice. "You don't have to do that."

"I want to, though. Why do you think I stayed up this late? Of course, I was hoping you'd be in a more...celebratory mood."

He leaned forward and gently brushed his mouth over Phil's. He responded by parting his lips, and Gregory repeated the caress, lingering a little longer on his warm skin. Each slow touch made the back of his neck tingle, but he didn't rush it. He took his time, coaxing soft sighs from Phillip's throat. The tip of his tongue danced over Phil's bottom lip, then teased the corner of his mouth. He wanted Phillip to be completely focused on his mouth, his tongue, the warmth of his breath. If Phil's mind strayed, even a little, the mood would be shattered.

Gregory finally broke when Phillip moaned with frustration. The sound sent a jolt to his groin, and he slid his tongue against Phil's, filling his mouth, forcing another moan, and another. Phillip cupped the back of his head, holding him with strong fingers as he deepened the kiss. Gregory's hand moved down Phil's body, seeking out his growing erection beneath the loose material of his boxers.

"God, you smell good," Phillip said against his mouth. "How come you always smell so good?"

"Don't know."

He moved his lips along Gregory's jaw and down his neck,

27

in hard, hungry kisses. "You taste so good too."

With a hand on Gregory's shoulder, Phillip pushed him flat on his back, half-covering his body. Gregory didn't take his hand from Phil's cock. He ran his fingers up and down the shaft, almost playfully, until Phil was completely erect. As soon as Greg closed his palm around his length, Phillip thrust his hips. Gregory responded with slow, even strokes, steadily building the friction.

"I've missed you so much," Phillip whispered. He lifted his head and cupped Gregory's face. "I feel like I've been there for everybody except you."

"That's not true."

"It is true. I didn't help you today."

"I didn't call you."

"If you had, I would have told you to call a tow truck. I didn't have time to come and help."

Gregory lifted his head and kissed Phillip tenderly. "I know you're busy. I don't hold it against you."

"I want to show you that I..."

"I know. But you can show me anyway."

Phillip sat back on his heels and worked Gregory's shorts down his legs. Gregory always felt a little self-conscious when Phillip studied him—he didn't like to be under scrutiny. They were about the same size when it came to clothes, but Gregory was just skinny. Almost awkwardly so. Phillip was *fit*. Fastest-mile-in-department-history *fit*. The best at any sport he ever tried from fencing to football *fit*. But Phillip never acted like Gregory's body left anything to be desired.

The first swipe of Phillip's tongue across Gregory's cock made him jerk off the mattress. Phillip hooked an arm under Gregory's leg and pulled it up and over Phil's head, then settled between his thighs, his mouth returning to Gregory's cock. He knew every sensitive spot on Gregory's body and knew how to exploit those sensitive spots. He could have Gregory twisted in a million knots, begging and shouting for relief. Or he could have Gregory completely lax and mindless on the bed, too lost in pleasure to voice a single demand. Phillip was thorough. Now he teased Gregory until he was throbbing everywhere—his cock, his balls, his groin, his ass, his toes, even behind his eyes.

Phillip didn't linger on Gregory's erection, though. He slowly made his way down, pausing to lick and nibble and suck at his balls and his thighs. And then his tongue was teasing Gregory's clenched hole, gently licking the tender muscle. He circled the pucker again and again, wetting it, preparing it for penetration of Phillip's finger.

"Oh!" Gregory jerked his hips, encouraging more. A second finger quickly joined the first one, stretching Gregory's flesh, preparing it for Phil's cock. His mouth came down on Gregory's balls. Each touch of his tongue, each scrape of his teeth, the pressure of his lips, the vibrations from his moans, sent shivers and flashes through Gregory's body.

"Christ, Phil."

"Hmm?"

"I'm ready." Phillip hit his prostate and sent a shockwave up Gregory's spine. "Very ready. Please."

His fingers and mouth disappeared, but that didn't matter. Gregory still felt him. He always felt Phil, the ghosts of his mouth and hands coasting over his body. He heard Phillip fumble for the lubricant, heard the snap of the lid as he popped it open with his thumb, then the soft sigh as he poured the cool liquid over his heated skin.

"You sure you're ready?"

"Yes, yes. Please."

The blunt tip of his cock pressed against Gregory's slick skin, and then it was pushing into his body, deeper and deeper until Gregory thought he would break. Phillip fell forward, catching himself on his palms, and their mouths clashed, their tongues dueling as Phillip moved his hips in slow, purposeful thrusts. Closing his eyes, Gregory wrapped his arms and legs around his lover. They clung together, their bodies sliding against each other in an easy, familiar rhythm.

"That's it," Gregory murmured. "That's it...fuck...don't stop...please don't stop...Phil...please..."

"Love you," Phillip panted, the words almost lost in the sound of flesh slapping against flesh. His skin was slick and heated against Gregory's, and his neck tasted salty every time Gregory caught him with his lips and tongue.

The orgasm was a slow burn, winding through Gregory's veins. Phillip must have felt him stiffen as he arched from the bed, because he reached between their bodies to grip Gregory's cock. He stroked it in time with his thrusts, and the pressure against his prostate combined with the force of Phillip's hand made him cry out. He coated their chests with his come, and clenched around Phillip's cock. Phil shuddered above him, and then string after string of his jizz filled Gregory's ass.

Phillip chased a bead of sweat across Gregory's brow, his lips coming to rest at his temple. "Thank you."

Greg sighed. "I think I should be thanking you. Now try to get some sleep."

"I'll try."

Phillip rolled off him and onto his back. Gregory settled on his side, his head resting on Phil's shoulder. His eyes were heavy. He wanted to be sure Phillip rested, but he couldn't resist closing his eyes, or the soft pull of sleep.

Chapter Two

"What is that sound?" Phillip asked, without lifting his head from the pillow.

Gregory cracked an eyelid open enough to ascertain that it was midmorning. "What sound?"

He was answered by a steady *thump thump*. Like somebody pounding on the...

"That sound," Phillip said. "It's somebody at the door."

"Oh."

"Are you going to answer it?"

"No."

"That's fine then."

Gregory dropped his head back to the pillow and closed his eyes. He couldn't force himself out of bed. Not with Phillip spooning him and the sun caressing his face. He wanted to wake up slowly, and then turn over and get his mouth around Phil's morning erection.

Except the knocking returned.

"Were you expecting somebody?" Phillip muttered.

"No. Why would I expect somebody on a Sunday morning?"

"I heard there were some Mormons in the neighborhood."

"You think it might be them?"

"Who else would it be on a Sunday morning?"

"I can't argue with that logic." Gregory rolled out of bed. "I'll go get rid of them."

"You're not going to get dressed?"

"I'll give the lads a thrill."

Gregory stumbled out of the bedroom, his eyes still half shut. The clock that hung above the stairs chimed eight times as he walked. Eight wasn't a very good lie-in, as far as Gregory was concerned. The descent to the front door was slow going because he hadn't grabbed his glasses, and the world was an interesting blur, broken up occasionally by solid objects inches from his face.

He threw the door open without checking the peephole first. The world swam in front of his tired eyes, but not before he noticed that there wasn't a pair of young men standing on his stoop. It was only one man. And he wasn't holding a Bible. He was holding a brown paper sack.

"Well, good morning to you too," said a familiar, laughing voice.

"Oh...bloody hell."

Gregory tried to slam the door, but Jim put his hand out and stopped it before it met his face. "Now, that *is* British for fuck, right?"

"No, fuck is British for fuck," Gregory muttered, ripping a jacket from a nearby hook and tying it around his waist. "What are you doing here?"

"I'm bringing you breakfast."

"Why are you bringing me breakfast?"

Jim pushed the door open further and stepped into the house. "I thought you might like some. I also thought I'd find you out in the garden."

"Why?"

"I thought you mentioned that you two worked in the flowerbed."

"Who is it?" Phillip shouted from the top of the stairs.

"Jim."

"Jim?"

"We were staying in bed this morning," Gregory explained.

Jim dragged his gaze up and down Gregory's body. His pulse quickened at the frank appraisal. For a moment—for a mere second—he forgot Phillip was waiting upstairs. The world zeroed in to Jim Tennant's hazel eyes, his golden hair, his white smile, and in turn, Gregory felt like the only person on the planet. He was the only person who mattered, because he was the only one Jim was smiling at.

"Did I interrupt anything?"

"What? No. No, we were asleep."

"Late night?"

"Phillip didn't get in until after three."

"Oh, I'm sorry. Why don't we let him sleep and share these sausage rolls?"

"I'll...I'll go upstairs and see if he wants to come down and join us."

Judging from the look on Phillip's face, he did not want to join them. Gregory quietly shut the door behind him and smiled apologetically. "I didn't know he was going to show up."

"You didn't invite him? Or mention seeing him again?"

"No. We shared a few pints, he walked me home, and that was the end of that."

"Clearly not."

Gregory ran his fingers over the ridge of Phil's shoulder.

"Why don't you come downstairs and have breakfast with us? He's a nice guy. I don't think he meant anything by coming over this morning. Maybe that's a common American thing."

Phillip snorted. "No, I'm sure this is rude wherever you're from."

"Come down to breakfast anyway."

"Fine. But then we're sending him away."

"I can live with that."

"With the understanding that he's not to show up here unannounced or uninvited again."

"Absolutely."

Phillip kissed the corner of his mouth. "Then I guess we better not keep our guest waiting."

Gregory dressed quickly, excited to get back downstairs. He wasn't sure the source of his excitement, and he wasn't sure he wanted to think about it, either. But now that he was more awake, and dressed, he thought he wouldn't mind being on the receiving end of another of Jim's smiles.

Gregory found him in the kitchen, staring at Phillip's kettle with a look of confusion. "I still haven't figured out the whole tea thing."

"We drink coffee in the morning."

"You do?"

Gregory pointed to the coffeepot. "I'll get it started."

"Is Phillip coming downstairs?"

"He'll be down in a bit."

Gregory filled the coffeepot, studying Jim from the corner of his eye. He looked at ease. Not just at ease. He looked like he owned the entire kitchen, and Gregory was the interloper. He had the feeling that was how Jim Tennant moved through life. It was the sort of comfort and grace Gregory never felt in his own surroundings.

"Do you usually answer the door in your birthday suit?"

Warmth crawled up Gregory's neck. "No. I thought you were..."

"Who?"

He kept his eyes trained on the coffeepot. "Missionaries."

"You were going to flash *missionaries*?"

"I know. It's awful. It seemed like a good idea when I was half-asleep."

"Are you kidding?" Jim chuckled. "I think that's the best idea I ever heard. Maybe I should pretend to be a missionary more often."

"Nobody would believe you're a missionary."

"What's that?"

"You're not exactly a choirboy, are you?"

Jim leaned against the counter, his long legs stretched in front of him. "I actually *was* a choirboy. Do you believe me?"

"No."

"Would a choirboy lie to you?"

"I don't know what you'd do. I don't really know you that well, do I?"

"You know me well enough to have breakfast with me."

Gregory shook his head. "You're lucky I answered the door and not Phillip. He's not so tolerant of strange men coming around on Sunday mornings."

Jim turned to face Gregory, propping himself up on his arm. "I'm not a strange man."

"Yes. You are."

"We spent most of yesterday together."

"You could have been lying to me most of yesterday too." Gregory flipped the coffeepot on. "We never discussed having breakfast plans, did we?"

"I was hoping you'd find breakfast with me so enjoyable, you'd agree to do it again sometime."

Gregory turned away from him to open the fridge. The innuendo seemed obvious, but at the same time, who would have the sheer gall to make sexually suggestive comments to a man while his lover was in the house? It was too insane to consider. Not realistically, anyway.

"Gregory isn't a big fan of breakfast," Phillip said as he entered the room.

"Didn't anybody ever tell him that breakfast was the most important meal of the day?"

"I guess not."

Gregory took three mugs from the cupboard.

Jim shrugged. "Maybe he doesn't work up enough of an appetite at night."

Gregory opened his mouth, but before he said anything, Phillip cut in. "No, it's not that."

There was a long pause. Gregory didn't turn around, but he imagined Jim's gaze traveling up and down Phillip's body, the same way it had raked over his form earlier. "No, I guess it wouldn't be that."

The drawl in his voice made Gregory shiver. He glanced over his shoulder to see if it affected Phillip the same way, but his lover's face was as impassive as ever. Of course, he'd be impassive to it. Phillip wasn't as easily swayed, or impressed, as mere mortals.

"So, Mr. Tennant, where do you live?" Phillip asked.

"It's Jim, please. And I actually don't live too far from here, as luck would have it."

"And you don't have any friends or family to pester on Sunday mornings?"

Gregory looked up sharply. "Phil."

Jim laughed. "It's a fair enough question. No, I haven't. I moved here from California. Really, just last weekend."

Gregory felt a stab of sympathy for Jim. He would never have the fortitude to pick up and move to the other side of a planet. Not by himself. Even if he got over the fear of flying, living alone would be far too daunting.

"Gregory was the first friendly face I've met since I arrived in England."

Gregory poured three cups of coffee. "Do you take cream or sugar?"

"No. Just black, please."

"You sure?"

"Very sure."

Phillip accepted his coffee from Gregory—with two sugars and no cream—and smiled a little. "Gregory was the first friendly face I met when I moved here too."

"Is that so?" Jim took his coffee and sipped from the mug. "Did you rescue him on the side of the road too?"

"No. I arrested him."

Jim nearly spit out his coffee, and Gregory smiled sheepishly. "I was in the wrong place at the wrong time."

"That's true."

"So..." The devilish twinkle was back in Jim's eye. "Did he find a way to bribe his way into freedom?"

Gregory winced internally. The hint of corruption was usually enough to offend Phillip. He knew Jim was teasing but...

"He didn't have the chance," Phillip said lightly. "I released him and invited him to dinner."

The coffee burned Gregory's tongue, even with the generous serving of milk he added to cool it. Phillip crossed the room to Jim's side, reaching for the brown paper sack. They stood shoulder to shoulder for a brief moment, but it was long enough for each detail to be imprinted to Gregory's memory. Phillip looked like snow next to Jim. His white-blond hair, his pale skin, his blue T-shirt, all washed out next to the strong, golden hue of Jim's skin. The contrast reminded Gregory of a midwinter day, when the sun glinted off the ice.

He pulled himself out of his thoughts and took out three plates, then set them on the counter in front of Phillip.

"You're quiet this morning, Gregory," Jim observed.

"Am I?"

"I guess you were more chatty yesterday."

"I'm still waking up," Gregory said, a little self-consciously.

"Do you know how difficult it is to find donuts around here? Seriously?"

"Donuts?" Phillip asked, biting into his roll. "For what? Breakfast?"

"Yeah. There's nothing like biting into a fresh, warm donut."

"They're too sweet for me," Phillip said. "I prefer sausage."

Jim grinned. A slow, knowing grin. "I suppose sausage definitely has its advantages."

"If you want donuts for breakfast," Gregory cut in, "there's a bakery that has them on the weekends. I don't know if they'll be as good as you're used to, but I can give you the address."

"Thanks, Greg. I'd appreciate that."

"Do you want to sit down?" Phillip asked, nodding at the small, round table. There were only two chairs, but Phil lifted himself onto the counter, letting his legs dangle at the side, and leaving Gregory to sit with Jim.

"I was thinking about what you said yesterday," Jim started, his gaze on the dark liquid in his cup.

"I don't know which thing you're referring to. We talked a lot."

"About the flowers."

Gregory caught Phil's gaze over Jim's shoulder. Phillip arched his brow in a silent question. In response, Greg lifted his shoulder in a half-shrug.

"What about the flowers?"

"How they help you focus. I live in an apartment...a flat, I guess. I don't have a yard there."

The confusion on Phillip's face deepened. Gregory's face must have mirrored his, but he thought their confusion might have stemmed from different places. Phillip no doubt wanted to know why somebody like Jim Tennant would be interested in his garden. Gregory was wondering why Jim had such a hard time asking for what he wanted.

"I never had a garden until I moved in with Phillip," Gregory said. "Course, I never knew I wanted one until I moved in with Phillip."

"Did you have one, Jim? In America?" Phillip asked, with mingled curiosity and politeness.

"What? No. Well, sort of. I guess. I grew up on a farm, but after I left home, I've been bouncing from apartment to apartment."

"You can stay, if you want. We'll weed for an hour, it'll kill your back, and you'll never want to fuss with one again,"

Gregory said.

Jim's smile immediately returned. Gregory thought he would give Jim the entire garden, and the house, to see him smile like that again. But he felt Phillip's heavy eyes on him, and he quickly looked away from Jim. The last thing he wanted to do was swoon like some teenage girl over Jim in front of his boyfriend.

"I appreciate the invitation. Especially since I would have figured out a way to stick around either way."

Gregory grinned. "I know you would have."

"Does that bother you?"

"Do I look bothered?"

Jim leaned over the table, somehow narrowing the world to the two of them. "You look like you want me to stay."

"Well, I don't want you to be lonely."

"You're very thoughtful. That's what I like about you."

"That's the only thing, I hope."

"When it comes to you, I can't narrow it down to one thing."

Gregory sat back and forced himself to break eye contact, sipping from his coffee to disguise his discomfort. Tentatively, he looked over Jim's shoulder to meet Phil's eyes, expecting to see anger on his familiar face. But he looked...intrigued. Like he was watching an interesting play, and he wanted to see what happened in the next act.

"Do we...have a spare pair of gloves?" Gregory asked, hoping he didn't sound too lame.

"We should, out in the shed."

Gregory sucked down his coffee as fast as he dared and pushed away from the table. "I'll go see if I can find them."

He didn't give either of the other men a chance to protest

before he fled, but it did occur to him that something bad could happen if he left Phillip and Jim alone. Phillip wasn't the jealous type, but Gregory had never given him any reason to be jealous before. Was he giving him a reason now?

Gregory found the extra set of gardening gloves, as well as a spade and a trowel, in case Jim intended to work. When he stepped out of the dim shed, his skin felt a little less tight, and his pulse was back to normal. He found Jim and Phillip in the garden, both of them kneeling in the dirt, and Phillip was pointing to his flowers.

"This is a sturdy plant. It's the first one I planted here and it's pretty hardy."

Gregory cared about the flowers because Phillip did, but Jim seemed genuinely interested in each plant, where it came from, what it needed to survive. The more Phillip talked about the garden, the more he relaxed, and Gregory was held in rapt attention. He wasn't the only one. Jim didn't cut in with questions, didn't try to flirt, and his eyes were serious.

Gregory hoped that Jim would see Phillip like he did. So few people had the chance to see Phillip in his element. Gregory wasn't sure why it was so important for Jim to know Phillip, to really *appreciate* Phillip. Like Jim was already a regular part of their lives.

Jim pulled a clump of weeds from the ground and laughed. Gregory sat back on his heels and stared up into the clear blue sky, imagining Jim taking his planes on their controlled falls. The thought frightened and excited him in equal parts.

Maybe Jim really was a part of their lives.

"You've done this before, you know."

Gregory looked up from the dish he was scrubbing. Jim had finally gone home, after promising—warning?—them that he would come by later that week. He wanted them to show him the sights of the city. When Phillip hadn't vetoed the idea, Gregory agreed without reservation. "What? Washed the dishes?"

"You know what I mean." Phillip folded his arms and rested his hip against the edge of the sink. Gregory pointedly focused on his task, avoiding Phil's blue eyes.

"I don't."

"You fall for people like Jim."

"I do not."

"Your ex was like him."

"I don't know what..." Gregory sighed. "Liam isn't anything like Jim Tennant."

"You like the way he flirts with you."

"I don't."

"You can admit it."

"Maybe I like it a little bit," Gregory muttered. He was still going through the motions of cleaning the plate, but he didn't think he was accomplishing anything. It seemed easier to keep his hands submerged in the hot, soapy water.

Phillip moved closer, crowding him. "Maybe more than a little bit."

"It's just some harmless flirting, Phil. I wouldn't...you know I would never let it move beyond that."

"Oh, I know." Phillip's mouth was right at his ear. "But if you didn't know me, you'd be with him right now, wouldn't you? Maybe on your knees for him."

Gregory shivered. The image itself was powerful, but it was the low cadence of Phillip's voice that hit him in the gut. Phillip slid his hand over Gregory's shoulder and down his chest. He didn't stop until his fingers brushed against the growing bulge in Gregory's pants.

"Isn't that right?"

"I..."

Phil squeezed his erection through the denim. "Don't lie to me, Greg. Don't ever do that."

"I won't," Gregory gasped. "I won't lie to you, Phil, I promise."

"Good boy," Phillip murmured, his breath hot against Gregory's skin. He rewarded Gregory for his promise by sliding the heel of his hand up and down Greg's shaft. Gregory's knees buckled and he leaned heavily on the counter, afraid he would fall to the ground if he didn't support his weight on something.

"Are you going to answer my question?"

How was he supposed to think? For a long second, he didn't even remember Phillip's question.

"I...I would be with him."

"That's what I thought." Phillip sidestepped and stood behind Gregory, pressing his erection against Gregory's ass. Greg was effectively pinned against the sink, Phillip being more than strong enough to hold him in place. His hand never left Gregory's shaft, and the rough denim added the exquisite friction Phil was building. "Why?"

Before Greg answered, Phillip kissed the back of his neck. Only, it wasn't quite a kiss. It was too hard, and Greg felt the sharp points of his lover's teeth graze his skin. But it wasn't a bite. It wasn't a nibble. It was demanding and hot. Despite the heat, goose bumps erupted on his neck and down his shoulders.

"Why?"

"Because he's gorgeous. Because he wants me and I like the way he looks at me."

"So, you have noticed it, then."

"Yes." Gregory dropped his head forward and reached behind him to grip Phil's hip. "Of course I have. He's not subtle. Are you mad?"

Phillip pushed against him, grinding his erection against Gregory. "Do I feel mad?"

Greg moaned. "No."

"I'll tell you a secret. I like it when other guys look at you. Because then I can think about all the ways they want you, and all the ways I can have you."

His stomach twisted into knots, and Phillip never stopped stroking him, never gave him a moment to catch his breath. He felt like he'd climb the walls, like the heat racing through his veins would simply erupt out of his skin. His mouth watered and his ass clenched, and every inch of him was ready for Phillip to stop teasing him, to bend him over the table and fuck him until he couldn't even catch his breath to beg for more.

"What do you want from him? Do you want him to fuck you? Do you want him to touch you like this? Do you want to suck his cock?"

"Yes." The shields between his brain and his mouth were gone, and Greg blurted the answer without hesitation. "I want to get on my knees for him. I want him to fuck my mouth."

The teeth on his tender earlobe pulled a sharp groan from Greg. "Is that so?"

"Yes."

"Did you want to suck his cock yesterday when you went

out to the pub?"

"Yes." He was past the point of knowing the truth from a lie. He didn't know where his hunger for Phillip began and ended, or where it overlapped with his attraction to Jim.

"Would you have done it?" More pressure on his cock, like Phillip wanted to break him.

"No..."

"Would you have done it if he asked you?"

The thought of Jim asking Greg to go down on him sent a sharp, dizzying stab of lust through his body. He almost heard the words, almost saw the light in Jim's eyes.

"No, I..."

Teeth on his neck. Phillip's strong arm around his body, holding him like he never intended to let him go. And then Phillip's low, coaxing voice. "Tell me the truth, Greg."

"God...yes. In a second."

Phillip suddenly released him, and Gregory froze. Had he misunderstood? Had he answered wrong? Did Phillip want him to deny it? A hand on his elbow pulled him from his thoughts, and two soft words banished his doubts and insecurities, and heightened his already painful desire.

"Show me."

Gregory turned and dropped to his knees without further prompting. Phillip unzipped his jeans slowly, then pulled his stiff cock out for Gregory's hands and mouth.

"I want you to show me what you would do if he asked."

Gregory's scalp tightened and tingled, and his tongue felt thick and hungry. For a moment, Phillip was Jim Tennant. And for a moment, Gregory was a man who would forget his commitments, who would ignore his better feelings to give into a baser, primal hunger. He'd never be that man, but at that moment, the shared fantasy was too powerful to ignore.

Gregory parted his lips and sucked the tip of Phil's cock into his mouth. It was already wet with pre-come, the salty liquid coating his lips and tongue. The evidence of Phillip's arousal added new knots to his stomach. His own cock jerked in the tight constraint of his jeans, but he didn't take his hands away from Phillip's body. The restriction, the lack of contact, made the tightness better.

"I want to see how hungry you are for it."

Gregory closed his eyes, letting his mind transport him. He was in the front seat of his car, parked outside Jim's flat, his cock throbbing from the proximity and the smell of Jim's skin. Jim had just kissed him, and he was asking Gregory for more. Asking with his eyes. Nobody would know. Phillip would never know if Greg leaned over, unzipped Jim's pants, and swallowed him.

"Yes," Phillip hissed.

Gregory gripped Phil's ass with both hands, his fingers digging into the flesh as he sank lower on his shaft. He didn't stop when the head of Phil's cock met resistance at the back of his throat. He wouldn't stop at that point if he were getting Jim off in the car, after all. He suppressed his gag reflex and kept swallowing, until his lips were wrapped around Phil's shaft, and his throat was full with his cock.

"That's it. Oh, that's it, Greg...let me see how much you want it..."

Gregory held his position for a few moments and then pulled back. He knew Phillip liked a slow, steady rhythm. He always wanted a slow build, and Gregory had shaped his technique over the years to fulfill that need. But Jim wouldn't want a slow, steady buildup. Jim would want him to move hard and furious. And Phillip's soft words of encouragement told him to give in to that impulse.

He gripped the base of Phillip's shaft and began to move his head in fast, even strokes. Each time he pulled back, he stroked upward with his hand, then he followed his fist down Phil's length with his mouth. His tongue moved around and over and down and up, and he wasn't shy about letting his teeth brush against Phil's tight skin. Despite the fantasy unfolding in Gregory's brain, the taste and smell of Phil, the warmth in his skin, the pulse throbbing against his lips, were simply bliss.

"That's it. God, Greg. Don't stop. Don't…"

Gregory's other hand went to Phil's balls, and he cupped the sac with as much force as he knew Phillip could stand. As soon as he flexed his fingers, Phil's palm went to the back of Gregory's head, holding him in place. Greg didn't resist his strong fingers. He stopped right where Phil wanted him to stop and let him pound into his mouth. Seconds or minutes might have passed. Gregory lost track. The only thing that mattered was the way Phillip stretched his throat again and again and again.

"Oh, Greg, I'm going to…"

He pulled his cock free from Gregory's lips and stroked his shaft once before he erupted, letting his come coat Gregory's cheek, lips and tongue. Greg sighed as the warm liquid splashed against his skin and rolled down his jaw. Before Greg licked his skin clean, Phillip dropped to his knees and claimed his mouth in a hard kiss.

Gregory's body was still thrumming with desire, his mind still in the middle of the fantasy Phillip set up.

"Don't stop talking," he begged against Phil's lips.

"I won't." He dragged his mouth to Gregory's cheek, lapping the strings of jizz from his cheek. "Where were you?"

"The car."

Phillip yanked at his zipper, and Gregory cried out as Phil finally freed his cock. His fingers were hot and perfect around Greg's shaft, and Phil stripped Gregory's cock, moving his wrist in hard, relentless strokes.

"Do you want to ride him? Climb onto that big dick of his and let him split you in two?"

"Oh...yes."

"You would have had the perfect excuse. You were too drunk to know better, and nobody else would ever know. Think about that, Greg. Think about how he could have spent all night fucking you."

Gregory did think about it. Jim's body would flex and pulse as Greg sank on his slick cock. He'd ride Jim with the promise that it would never happen again. Until Jim whispered in his ear, begging Greg to come upstairs with him, begging Greg to spend the night so he could fuck him against every hard surface in the flat.

The base of his spine tingled a split second before the orgasm detonated and rolled through his body. Phillip found his mouth again and swallowed Gregory's loud moans, kissing him until his cock stopped jerking.

"You okay?" Phil murmured.

"I wish you'd warn me before you do that."

"Half the fun is the surprise, isn't it?"

Gregory snorted. "I guess so."

"You had fun, right?"

"I think the evidence is all over your hand."

"I didn't make you uncomfortable, did I?"

Gregory rested his brow against Phil's. "Why would you say that?"

"Because I think you were telling the truth."

Gregory reared back. "Phillip, you know I would never..."

Phillip cupped the side of his face. "I know you wouldn't. You know you're pretty much the only person I trust implicitly. But you're human, Gregory. And people respond to flirting and attraction."

"I guess some of it was true. I do like the way he looks at me. I am attracted to him."

"See? I can trust you because you always tell me the truth."

"You know what else is true?"

"What?"

"I'm completely in love with you."

Phillip smiled. "Yeah, I know. Why don't we save these dishes for later?"

Gregory arched his brow. "You, Phillip Baker, are suggesting we leave dirty dishes in the sink until an undefined point in the future? Really? I didn't literally suck your brains out, did I?"

Phil's laugh warmed Gregory through his chest. "Tonight is my last day off for, what, a week or more? I want to make the most of it. You're not complaining, are you?"

"I wouldn't dream of complaining. I'm scared you'll change your mind if I do."

Phillip straightened and pulled Gregory to his feet. "Can I tell you the truth about something?"

"What?"

"I understand why you're attracted to him."

"He got under your skin too?"

Phillip took his hand and guided him out of the kitchen. "A little bit. There's something about him. For all his arrogance..."

"And he has a lot of arrogance."

"Yes. Did you notice he doesn't walk? He sort of swaggers."

Gregory chuckled. "I noticed. Anyway, you were saying that for all his arrogance?"

"Oh. I think he's missing something, but he doesn't know what it is."

"And why am I not surprised you want to fix him?"

"Hey. I don't need a project. You didn't need to be *fixed*, did you?"

"Well, that's where you're wrong. I very much needed you to fix me." Gregory brought Phillip's hand up to his lips. "And you did."

Chapter Three

Gregory opened the door and didn't even try to disguise his pleased smile. "Where the hell have you been?"

Jim looked almost sheepish at the question. "My job isn't all fun and games. I have a lot of paperwork to do."

"I guess so, if it takes a week."

"What are you up to? Can you go out for a beer?"

Gregory shook his head. "I'm cooking Phillip dinner tonight."

Jim perked up at the mention of dinner. "Can I help?"

"Do you know how to cook?"

"Can you show me?"

Gregory laughed. "I can try. Come on in."

"What's for dinner?"

"My very special lasagna. I've got the noodles boiled, now I'm working on putting everything together."

Jim arched his brow. "This is real lasagna, right? And not what passes for lasagna in this place?"

"The way you talk makes me think you've had some bad experiences."

"To put it mildly."

"A little homesick?"

Jim shrugged. "I guess you could say that. Not that being in England is all bad. The company makes up for the lack of good food."

"I'll make sure you have good food and good company tonight. Come on."

He was relieved Jim had shown up unannounced, because he had been considering calling the other man himself. The week since they last saw him had been oddly quiet—almost too quiet. Gregory missed Jim's teasing smile, and his hazel eyes, and the tone of his voice when he said something that bordered on inappropriate.

"So, Phillip won't be working till all hours of the night?"

"Not tonight. Well, hopefully. He hasn't called me yet to tell me he's going to be late, so I'm going to assume that he'll be here." Gregory beckoned Jim over to the stove. "Don't let this sausage burn."

Jim eyed the two pans on the stovetop. The other was at a merry simmer. "You make your own sauce even?"

"It's a special treat."

"How special?" Jim frowned. "I'm not interrupting an anniversary or birthday or something, am I?"

"No, not at all. I just felt like making lasagna."

"I have a confession to make."

"I would imagine you had more than one." Gregory kept his voice light, though Jim's declaration had sounded uncharacteristically solemn. He layered the bottom of the baking pan with noodles, concentrating on lining up the wide noodles exactly so he wouldn't have to focus on Jim.

"That's true. But for right now, my confession is that I wouldn't care if tonight was your anniversary. I still wouldn't leave."

"Why not?"

And then Jim was standing behind him, instead of tending to the sausage. "Because I missed you this week."

"You did?"

Jim gripped his shoulders, though that was the only contact. Gregory still felt the space between his back and Jim's chest. "You were all I thought about this week. And my thoughts weren't very platonic."

"Jim, I..."

"I know. You're with Phillip. The two of you are very happy together. I don't want to come between the two of you. Well, no. I guess the problem is that's exactly what I want."

"Jim, we're friends." Gregory was proud of himself for keeping the words more or less even. They were just friends. That's all they could ever be.

"I know. But do you know what I would do if we weren't just friends?"

Gregory shook his head, even though he had a good idea of what the answer would be. Despite the heavy scent of garlic, onions and sausage, he smelled Jim's cologne. He realized Jim was barely holding him. If he wanted to get away, he could. If he wanted to push him back and put the entire distance of the room between them, he could.

"Can I show you?" He gently turned Gregory around to face him, and Gregory allowed it. It was harder to concentrate with Jim's eyes boring into his. Jim was hypnotizing him. He didn't know how. He didn't know why. But he knew it was happening. "Just once?"

"I can't." The protest was undermined by the weakness in his throat. It sounded like nothing more than a token refusal. But it was much more than that. So much more than that.

"Just once," Jim repeated, tilting his head. He licked his lips, and Gregory followed the motion with his eyes.

"No." He emphasized his refusal by pushing Jim away. "It's not going to happen."

Jim looked shock, then hurt, and then sorry. "I'm sorry. I shouldn't have done that. I..." He shook his head. "I don't have an excuse. Do you want me to go?"

"You don't have to go. I missed you this week too. Unless...being friends isn't enough."

"It's enough. Answer one question for me, okay?"

"What?"

"It's not only me, is it? You feel this...this thing between us."

"I feel it," Gregory conceded. "But that's just...attraction. I love Phillip."

"I guess it's my bad luck to find an honest man, isn't it?"

Gregory smiled slightly. "I guess so. Are you going to stay for dinner?"

"Yes."

"Are you going to keep your hands to yourself?"

"The most I can promise is to try."

"I guess that's good enough for me," Gregory said, turning back to his pan. Jim went back to the stove. Everything was back to normal.

Nothing was back to normal.

They couldn't turn the clock back five minutes, even if they both tried to pretend it didn't happen. Gregory wouldn't be able to forget it happened. He wouldn't be able to stop hoping it had happened. And he couldn't stop imagining how Jim's lips would fit against his own.

"Where did you learn how to make lasagna, anyway?"

Gregory blinked and had to run the question through his mind twice more to even understand the words.

"The woman who watched me when I was a kid was Italian. She taught me a lot about cooking."

"And you remember all that?"

"Well, I got a refresher course when I was in my early twenties. She was sick, and I stayed with her on the weekends. I think she was disappointed she didn't have her own children to pass the secrets down to."

"So she gave them to you."

"Yes."

"Who will you give them to?"

"I don't know. It'll be a shame if they end with me. She taught me how to make a lot of different recipes."

"Maybe you can teach me."

Gregory smiled a little sadly. "Yeah, maybe I can."

"I thought I told you not to do that," Jim said with forced lightness.

"Do what?"

"Agree to something because you think it'll make me happy to hear it."

"How do you know I was doing that?"

"Because I made you uncomfortable, and now you're trying to let me down gently. Not only are you honest, you're too good-hearted."

Gregory took a deep breath. "Can you do me a favor?"

"Name it."

"Run down to the store on the corner and buy some wine."

"Any kind in particular?"

"Anything that's cheap." Gregory turned to face him. "Buy a lot of it."

Jim's brows knitted together in a frown. "Any particular reason why you want a lot of wine?"

"I feel like drinking tonight. Don't you?"

"I never turn down a night of drinking, personally. That would be a bad habit to get into. But you don't strike me as somebody who drinks a lot. And I doubt Phillip is a big drinker."

"He's not." Gregory closed the distance between them. "But sometimes..."

Jim remained still, letting Gregory come to him. "What happens when you drink? Some people...act a little out of character."

"I've been known to get a little grabby, at times."

"Then it's probably not safe to drink with me. I'm not much of a gentleman."

"Phillip will be here."

"What's he going to do?"

"Make sure I don't get too grabby, I suppose."

Jim tilted his head, like he planned to steal the kiss denied him before. For a moment, Gregory thought he would let him. But then he was smiling, and stepping back, putting a safe amount of distance between them. "I'll be back with a couple of bottles."

"I'll be waiting."

The lasagna was excellent. Gregory barely tasted it, but Phillip and Jim both seemed to love it. They raved and both took second and then third helpings. Jim kept the cheap wine flowing, and Gregory lost track of how many glasses he downed. Jim didn't make any more advances, and if Phillip sensed any tension between the two of them, he didn't let on.

Gregory thought he sensed tension between them. Or he might have imagined it. Did he hurt Jim with his rejection? It didn't seem possible. Jim could waltz out of their house and pick up any number of people to soothe his broken heart. Not that Gregory had such a high opinion of himself. He never broke anybody's heart.

He studied Phillip through his lashes. And he never would, if he could help it.

After Phillip and Jim cleaned their plates—and Gregory made a show of finishing his first helping—they retired to the front room with the wine. Even Phillip indulged in a glass, though as soon as he sipped the dark liquid, he grimaced.

"What is this? The cheapest wine available?"

"Yes," Jim answered.

"Why?"

"Because that's what Gregory told me to buy."

Phillip's frown deepened. "Why?"

Gregory shrugged. "To stretch his money further."

"How much have you had to drink so far?"

Gregory shrugged again. He stopped keeping track after they shared the first bottle. There were still three more chilling in the fridge. "A few glasses."

Jim stood. "Speaking of drinking, I've got to hit the head."

Phillip gestured towards the hallway. "First door past the stairs."

Jim sauntered—swaggered—out of the room. Gregory stared. How could a man move that way?

Pepper Espinoza

"What's going on, Greg?"

Gregory dragged his attention back to Phillip. "Jim...tried to kiss me today."

"Tried?"

"He asked. I wouldn't let him."

"He *asked*?"

"Why is that so hard to believe?"

"I expected he wouldn't have worried about formalities."

Gregory felt cloudy and raw. "What are you saying? That you expected him to kiss me?"

"He looks at you like he could eat you alive."

He leaned forward. "I don't understand. Usually...look, remember when that bloke, Kevin, started looking at me like that? You laid him flat."

"This is different."

"Why?"

Phillip closed the distance between them, brushing Gregory's ear with his lips. Each bit of contact made Greg shiver, and he wrapped his arms around Phillip's body. He wanted to stay there, feeling warm and secure, for the rest of the night. The alcohol sloshed in his stomach, and he realized he was getting grabby. He wanted to nuzzle Phillip's neck, and then his chest, and then his cock.

"Because I think you two would be beautiful together."

Gregory reeled back. "What?"

"You think you're the only one attracted to him? Or the only one who enjoys the fantasy?"

"Yes."

Phillip gripped the back of Gregory's neck and pulled him closer. "I'm saying that if you want something from him...that's

58

fine. If you don't, that's fine too."

"I...but I don't want you to..."

"You don't have to do anything."

Greg lowered his gaze. "But I want to. It's not worth it to me—none of it's worth it to me—if you're hurt. Or unhappy."

"What did he ask you for earlier?"

"A kiss," Jim said from behind them.

They both looked up, and Greg felt a slow blush crawl up his neck and cheeks. How much had he overheard? Judging from the light in Jim's eyes, he had heard enough. More than enough. And with the taste of wine in the back of his throat, the hungry look on Jim's face, and Phillip's words echoing in his head, he didn't think he'd have the ability—or the desire—to resist Jim a second time.

"I already told you once that I don't want to come between the two of you, Greg. That's not what I'm interested in."

"What are you interested in?" Gregory whispered.

"Sharing you."

I could be dreaming. This could be a dream.

Or some sort of plot? A joke?

He couldn't say for sure about Jim, but he knew Phillip would never *joke* like this. It would be too cruel. And Phillip, for all of his stuffy and almost prudish behavior, loved to find ways to drive Gregory crazy. It seemed to be his most secret pleasure. But until that moment, Gregory never had any idea of how deep the pleasure ran for Phillip, or how far he was willing to take it.

"Phillip?"

Phillip shook his head. "Don't ask me, Greg. I think this all hinges on what you want."

It felt sinful. Gluttonous. That was the right sin. Gregory

hadn't gone to church in years, and Sunday school was far behind him, but indulging in this sort of shared fantasy was greedy. Though that was another sin, Gregory thought. Avarice. It was funny how closely those two sins were linked.

"Gregory?"

He looked up and smiled shyly. "Sorry."

"I think we might have broken his brain," Jim observed.

"I was thinking about...sins."

"You know what's more fun than thinking about them?" Jim rested his hands on the back of the sofa and leaned forward. "Actually committing some."

"Can I make one request?"

"Name it."

Gregory glanced over to Phillip. He was watching intently, but calmly. There were no telltale signs of anger in his eyes, no twitching of his brow, or thinning lips. He was just waiting to see what Gregory had to say, waiting to see what would unfold.

"I want that kiss. If it doesn't go well, no harm no foul. But if it does go well, then..." Gregory didn't have to finish his sentence. Phillip leaned forward slightly, and Jim's eyes danced.

"I can live with that," Jim promised.

Gregory braced himself as Jim leaned forward. He tried to tell himself that Jim could be a horrible kisser, that after all his fantasies and dreams, the whole experience could be steeped in disappointment. He tried to tell himself that, but he knew it was wrong, even before Jim's mouth actually met his.

There was a vaguely bitter sheen of wine on Jim's lips, and the smell of alcohol lingered on his breath. Greg kept his lips together, afraid of opening to the kiss too soon. Jim traced the seam of his mouth, teasing him lightly with the tip of his tongue. The patient coaxing finally forced Gregory to let Jim in, and a shiver went down his back at the first brush of their tongues. Jim gripped him by the shoulder, and deepened the kiss until he completely filled Gregory's world. There was nobody and nothing else, except Jim's demanding mouth, his clever tongue, the scrape of his teeth.

Gregory didn't want to let him go. He wanted to drag the other man down to the couch and devour his mouth until they were both winded and shaken. Desire spread through him, unfolding through his limbs, into his fingers and toes. His cock began to harden, and he knew that another kiss like this would have him stiff and aching.

They didn't break apart until Gregory's lungs burned. When Jim lifted his head, his eyes shone with an intensity Gregory had never seen from him. He couldn't look away. For a long beat his brain tried to process what happened. He finally dragged his gaze to Phillip, waiting to see if maybe he had changed his mind after that display.

But Gregory wasn't looking at a man who was unsure of what he wanted. And he wasn't looking at a jealous man, either. Phillip's lips were parted, and his pale cheeks were splotched with red. His blue eyes were vibrant. Gregory recognized that look. It was the look that compelled Gregory to crawl across the floor just to lick his salty skin.

"Did it go well?" Jim murmured.

"Yeah. Yeah, it did."

"Can I try one other thing?"

Gregory almost asked *what*, but then he decided he didn't care. Jim could do whatever he thought he needed to do. "Yes."

He tilted his head towards Phillip. Gregory watched, transfixed, as Jim's full lips met Phil's waiting mouth. He expected to feel a twinge—or maybe an entire jolt—of jealousy. But there wasn't anything like that. He didn't think for a second that Jim was interested in taking Phillip away from him, and Greg never doubted Phil's devotion to him. Gregory felt oddly detached from the scene, like they were enacting a moment they saw in a movie once, and at the same time, he felt incredibly connected. He knew what Jim's hot mouth felt like, overwhelming and hungry, and he felt Phil's response. Phil was a deliberate, careful person. He would read Jim for a few moments, assess what he was doing, and then carefully pitch his response to be just what the other man needed.

By the time Jim pulled away, Gregory's whole body throbbed. Only one thing would soothe that sort of ache, and that would be to agree to Jim's suggestion. He trusted Phil, if Phil trusted him.

"Good?" Gregory asked.

Jim licked his lips and smiled. "Very good. I knew you'd be tasty, but I didn't quite expect the same thing from Phil here. I guess I should have."

Gregory met Phil's eyes, and he smiled. "I could have you told how tasty he is, if you had asked."

"Let's move this upstairs," Phillip suggested as he stood. "It'll be more comfortable."

Gregory took Phillip's hand and let the other man pull him off the couch. Their fingers remained intertwined as they circled the couch, and Greg reached for Jim with his other hand, touching his arm, silently encouraging him to follow. Phillip led the way up the narrow stairs, with Jim behind them, and Greg reflected on how much he wanted to stay in the middle. With Phillip fucking his ass and Jim fucking his mouth, and then maybe he'd fuck Jim...

Gregory felt lightheaded at the thought. He still couldn't quite believe this was happening. But then they were in the bedroom, and Jim was closing the door behind them. He looked around and smiled.

"I don't think I've ever seen a bedroom so tidy."

Gregory snorted. "Are you surprised? You've seen the rest of the house."

"It makes me want to make a mess."

Phillip stepped behind Gregory, pressing against his back. Phil's cock was hard against his ass, and that more than anything convinced Gregory that he had nothing to worry about. Phil wrapped his arms around his shoulders and reached for the top button of Gregory's shirt, then popped it free. Jim stood out of touching distance, watching as Phillip worked down the line, exposing Gregory's body to Jim's hungry stare.

Greg didn't even have the chance to feel self-conscious. Jim looked like he wanted to attack Gregory with his mouth and not let up until they were both quivering and broken. Phillip stepped back to pull the shirt down his arms and discard it, then his hands went to Gregory's belt.

"May I?" Jim asked.

"Of course."

As soon as Jim stepped forward, Gregory closed his eyes. Not because he wanted to miss the desire on his face, but because he wanted to savor the way Jim smelled and the rough texture of his fingers scraping across his stomach before focusing on the belt. He tugged it free, and before Gregory had a chance to really think about what he was doing, the pants were unbuttoned and pulled down over his hips.

"Look at that."

Gregory opened his eyes, unsure of what Jim was talking about. He almost asked, but Jim's attention was focused on Gregory's erection—and he literally licked his lips.

"I feel a little underdressed here," Greg said, tugging at Jim's shirt. "I don't want to be the only one on display."

Jim yanked his shirt over his head and tossed it aside. "Not a problem."

Gregory stared. In any other situation, such a blatant display would have been rude. But Jim's body was perfect. Like Phillip, he looked to be fit enough to be the best and fastest at anything he tried—though he was much thicker than Phillip and had more muscle mass. Hair, slightly darker than the golden shade on his head, covered his chest, and his nipples were a dark pink against his tan skin. For a moment, Gregory forgot that he could touch, kiss, explore whatever he wanted, and he stood there, dumbly.

Until Phillip nudged him in the back.

That was all the encouragement Gregory needed. He bent his head and dragged his tongue over Jim's flat nipple, thrilling at the texture of his skin and the taste of his soap and his sweat. Jim moaned—it was an almost submissive sound. Like he could do nothing except stand there and accept what little scrap of attention Gregory wanted to throw his way.

But Gregory wanted to give him more than scraps.

He focused on Jim's pants without lifting his head, his tongue going over the dusky skin again and again as he worked his belt and fly open. The only thing that could pull Gregory's attention away from Jim's salty skin was the heavy cock against his palm, erect and smooth. His cock wasn't as long as Phil's, but it was a little wider, slightly bent to the right.

"God, Gregory. I've been thinking about this every night," Jim murmured.

The weight of his voice made Gregory weak. He wrapped his fingers around Jim's cock and stroked once, shivering at the satiny texture. Phillip stood behind him, his chest pressed against Gregory's bare back, his body a familiar shape, a familiar pressure. Phillip's chest was smoother than Jim's, and his nipples were hard. He felt Jim reach around him, resting his palms on Phillip's hips, creating a cage to trap Gregory in place.

The tip of his cock dragged across Jim's thigh, leaving a thread of sticky fluid on his skin. He felt Phillip's lips at his ear, and then, "Is your mouth watering for it?"

Gregory nodded.

"Then don't just stand there," Phillip encouraged.

Gregory looked up, meeting Jim's vibrant hazel eyes. He had never gazed at Gregory with such open hunger, and it made him feel a little light-headed. Greg remained locked in place, staring at Jim, getting lost in his eyes, until Jim cupped the back of his head. With a soft sigh, Jim leaned forward, and their mouths connected again. Jim didn't hold anything back from this caress. He didn't try to disguise his desire. He wasn't shy.

"Can we move to the bed?" Gregory murmured when Jim broke the kiss.

Jim glanced over Gregory's shoulder and then nodded. Phil never stopped touching Gregory's body as they moved to the large bed, but he paused and began to strip. Gregory knelt in the middle, reaching for Jim's hand to pull him onto the mattress. As soon as Jim joined him, their mouths came together again, and Gregory was lost in the sweet pressure of his lips.

But not so lost that he didn't notice when the mattress dipped as Phillip settled beside them. And then his familiar, clever mouth was on Gregory's chest, his tongue circling Greg's nipple. Sparks spiraled through Gregory's body, bouncing from his chest to his mouth and then back again. The two men were creating an electric current between them, and it sizzled through Gregory's body. Gregory didn't want it to stop any time soon.

He moved his mouth down Jim's body, marveling at each gasp and moan. Phillip pulled the same sort of sounds from Gregory, his mouth busy, his hands busier. After an exploration that wasn't as thorough as it could have been, Gregory reached Jim's thick cock. He closed his lips around the tip of Jim's cock, sucking the salty pre-come from the slit.

Jim ran his fingers through Gregory's hair. "What do you want? Do you want me to fuck you? Do you want to suck me while Phil fucks you?" He tugged gently on Greg's hair. "Do you want to fuck me?"

There were too many questions. Gregory didn't know how to answer any of them. It didn't help that Phillip was still using his mouth to find every single sensitive spot on Gregory's body.

"Answer him," Phillip encouraged, his lips forming the words against Gregory's skin. "Tell him what you want."

"Fuck me." Gregory blurted the words before he reconsidered them. "Fuck me, Jim. Please."

"Whatever you want, Greg. Phil?"

"Hmm?"

"Get him ready, please?"

The three of them shifted, repositioning themselves to form a new shape. Jim sat back on his heels at the top of the bed, his cock jutting proudly from between his thighs. Gregory settled on his hands and knees, his lips even with the top of Jim's shaft. And Phillip stretched out on his back, his long legs hanging off the side of the mattress, his head between Gregory's thighs. His fingers sought out Gregory's clenched hole as he sucked Gregory's balls against his tongue.

"Let me feel your mouth again," Jim breathed. "Please."

Gregory didn't need more encouragement to taste Jim's stiff cock. Another bead of pre-come glistened on the tip, and he licked it away. Each bit of the salty fluid made Gregory's mouth water. He wanted more. He wanted to taste Jim's come splash against his tongue, wanted to feel it running down his lips and chin, wanted Jim to lick the drops away from his skin.

"God, you feel better than I imagined." Jim ran his fingers through Gregory's hair, caressing his scalp, then the side of his face. His touch was light, encouraging without being demanding. "And I've been imagining this a lot. I won't lie to you. Since the day we met. You've got the most perfect mouth I've ever seen."

Phillip grunted. Maybe in approval. Maybe in agreement. One finger moved in and out of Gregory's body, and the thought of Phillip preparing him for another cock sent a sharp thrill down his spine. The understanding that Phillip would fill his throat while Jim fucked him made him shiver again. He wanted both men to pound into him until he lost himself completely. Until his body was nothing but quivering flesh, overwhelmed by the endless sensations, experiencing everything on the spectrum from pleasure to pain.

Phillip added a second finger and moved his wrist faster. The hot, wet suction around Gregory's balls made his cock leak, and he wondered if he would be able to hold back his orgasm, or if he would come as soon as Jim thrust into his waiting ass. He moaned, and swallowed more of Jim's cock, taking another inch and another, until his lips were nearly wrapped around the base.

"Gregory... Gregory..." Each soft moan made Greg ache. He rocked against Phillip's hand, encouraging him to go faster, trying to fulfill this overwhelming, nameless need that grew every time Jim spoke. "Come on, Greg...need to fuck you..."

Gregory lifted his head and gasped for breath. Jim gazed down to his flushed face and swollen lips, then bent and claimed his mouth. Phillip eased away from him as Jim continued the thorough caress, like he was chasing the taste of his own skin and pre-come. Gregory's fingers curled into the blanket, and he clung to the bed tightly, afraid if he let go he might slide off. The room tilted and twirled around him as the kiss continued—maybe all his blood was rushing to his groin. Or maybe Jim was stealing his breath, sucking the oxygen into his own lungs.

Jim finally looked up when Phillip crawled to the top of the bed. Gregory barely had the chance to inhale before Phillip demanded his mouth. Gregory gave into the kiss happily, their tongues dueling, their moans echoing each other's. He heard Jim rifling around in the nightstand, clearly looking for the lube and condoms. Gregory wanted to tell him where to find it, but when he attempted to pull back, Phillip chased him with his mouth, claiming Gregory's attention again before he spoke.

It turned out that Jim didn't need any directions from Gregory. By the time Phillip gave Gregory a chance to breathe, Jim had already slicked his ass with the cool lube. Gregory gasped and blinked, his vision a little blurry. When he opened his eyes again, Phil's cock was near his mouth, waiting for Gregory's attention.

"Are you ready?" Jim asked.

Gregory swallowed, despite the sudden tightness of his throat. He looked at Phillip through his lashes, searching his face one final time for any clue or hint that he didn't want this. As much as Gregory ached for Jim, he still knew that he would push him away and push him out of the house if that's what Phillip wanted. But Phillip merely nodded, giving him the same encouragement he had offered all night.

"I'm ready." Gregory glanced over his shoulder so he could see Jim's vibrant eyes. "I'm ready."

The blunt head of Jim's cock pressed against Gregory's stretched hole. Greg tried to relax, though his body was tight with anticipation. Jim didn't waste any time. He pushed into Gregory's body in a single, easy stroke, forcing his walls to stretch around his thick shaft.

"That's it," Jim murmured. "That's it. God, you feel amazing."

Gregory opened his mouth, perhaps intending to return the compliment, but Phillip took advantage of his parted lips and slid his cock into Greg's mouth. Gregory moaned at the contact and moved his mouth down his length. By the time Jim thrust forward again, Gregory was completely filled, pulsing around both cocks, shivering, flushed. Jim kept his pace slow at first, giving Gregory the chance to become fully adjusted to him, and he let Jim control the rhythm, rocking with his body. Phillip palmed the back of his head, forcing Gregory to take him all the way to his base each time he shifted forward.

The tempo felt perfect. Natural. Like the three of them could not have moved in any other way. Gregory's brain shut down, and his body responded on its own, following Jim's lead, remembering the perfect way to tongue Phillip's cock. And he was rewarded, not only with the deep satisfaction of feeling them both, but with moans, and sighs, and gasps. He loved the way they both sounded as their voices grew louder, an undeniable chorus of pleasure. Pleasure he was giving them. Pleasure they both deserved. Warmth suffused his body, spreading through him and then settling in his groin. His balls ached, and he had to reach between his legs to massage them, squeezing with firm fingers, flexing each time Jim thrust forward.

Gregory knew he was going to come first. Satisfaction raced through each vein, making his entire body throb with heat, stoked by the friction created between his body and Jim's. The sound of slick skin slapping against his flesh almost overwhelmed their groans and harsh shouts, and he felt like he was being pushed and pulled too many different directions. He was flesh and overheated blood. He didn't even have any breath. His skin would break open, to release the unbelievable pressure and to allow more pleasure to enter his body.

Gregory couldn't shout, though he wanted to. Instead, he made a dark, muffled sound around Phillip's thick shaft. Gregory's cock jerked, and then warm come coated his stomach and the bed. It seemed like he shot for long minutes, his body convulsing as soon as he thought he was finished. In reality, it had probably been seconds, but time had never felt so elastic before.

Phillip shouted his warning a mere second before he slammed forward, burying his cock in Gregory's throat. His come was hot on the back of Gregory's tongue, and he held his breath, his throat constricting as he swallowed each drop.

"Gregory!"

The sound ripped through Greg, and his body tensed, like he was going to reach another climax. But it was Jim's orgasm that swept through him, made him vibrate and shake. He felt it rolling through his body as Jim bent, stretching across Gregory's back. He felt Jim's heart thundering in his chest, and the slick heat of his skin. He gripped the sheet tighter, holding it until the aftershocks of the orgasm finally subsided.

"I never..."

Gregory waited for Jim to finish his sentence, but the thought hung between them, incomplete.

The three of them collapsed, and nobody spoke for a long

time. Gregory didn't know what to say, or what they needed to hear. He felt warm and tired. Sated.

"Do you want me to go?" Jim finally asked.

Gregory spoke first. "No."

"Just sleep," Phillip murmured.

Sleep. Gregory didn't want to sleep for too long. He still felt greedy for another round before Jim left their bed.

Chapter Four

"Jim is a late sleeper, isn't he?"

Phillip bit into his crisp bacon and offered a closed-mouth grin. "You wore him out," he said, after chasing his bacon with a sip of coffee.

"If anybody gets to have a lie-in, it's me."

"You have to work."

"With Jim in my bed, I'm tempted to call in sick."

Phillip pretended to pout. "You never called in sick for me."

"What about all those times I called in sick to nurse you back to health?"

"Doesn't count."

"My style of nursing usually includes blowjobs. It counts."

Phillip's grin widened. "Fine. I'll give you that one. But only because I want blowjobs the next time I get sick."

"Call in sick today, and you won't have to wait that long."

Phillip sighed. "I can't. I wish I could but..."

Gregory reached over the counter and squeezed his shoulder. "I know. I don't expect you to put Cambridge at risk just because there's a gorgeous man, naked and asleep, in our bed."

"I've had a lot of practice tearing myself away from gorgeous men, naked and asleep, in my bed."

Gregory arched his brow. "You mean your boyfriends on the side."

Phillip cupped the back of his head and drew him into a kiss. Phillip's breath tasted of mint and coffee, and he smelled the fresh soap and shaving cream on Phillip's skin. His stomach turned in a slow somersault at the familiar taste and scent, and he momentarily lost himself. He loved the way Phillip kissed him in the morning. And in the evening. And any other time Phillip felt like reminding him of what an amazing kisser he was.

"Now, Greg," he chided when he lifted his head, "you know I don't have time for any boyfriends on the side."

Gregory snorted. "Yeah, that's true. What do you want me to tell Jim when he wakes up?"

"Whatever you want to tell him."

"Well, what do you want to tell him? I mean, should I let him down gently? Should I invite him over for dinner tonight? Though, I suppose he doesn't want to hear anything, and this morning will be the last we see of him."

Phillip turned back to his breakfast. "I doubt it."

"Why?"

"Because you're amazing, and he's going to want his fill."

"His fill of me? No, he'll just want a turn at you. But you still haven't really answered my question."

"Use your best judgment, Greg. If it seems like he wants to come back, and you want him to come back, then there you go."

Phillip sounded very matter-of-fact, and Gregory believed he said exactly what he meant, but everything felt very uncertain to him. "What about rules?"

Phillip's lips twitched. "Rules?"

"Don't look at me like that. You like rules more than I do."

"I don't think so."

"Phillip, you've memorized the entire police handbook, all the addendums, and probably every law, too, for all I know. Your whole world is organized by rules. So now, I want to know the rules for this."

Phillip chewed thoughtfully. "Do you have any thoughts?"

"I have questions. What if I went upstairs after you went to work, and he wanted to pick up where he left off last night?"

"Is this a question or a fantasy?"

"I guess that depends on your answer, doesn't it?"

"Be honest with me, Gregory. Have fun with him. Enjoy yourself. But don't lie to me."

"This is very strange." Gregory ran his hands through Phillip's hair, trying to straighten it. "Fun, but very strange. Why haven't you tried to do anything like this before?"

"I never met anybody like Jim before."

"Would you have been interested in him if you had met him under different circumstances?"

"I don't know. Maybe. I haven't really given it much thought."

"I'll always be honest with you. And I do want to go upstairs and pick up where we left off last night. If Jim is interested, that is."

"Can we go out tonight? Just the two of us?"

Gregory leaned forward to kiss the corner of Phil's mouth. "Are you asking me out on a date?"

"Yes, sir. Would you do me the honor?"

"Name the time and place."

"Tonight. Nine o'clock." Phillip named a restaurant they

had never visited, though Gregory had always wanted to try it.

Gregory frowned. "Do you have reservations?"

"Yes."

"You...you actually made reservations at a nice restaurant? When was the last time that worked for us?"

"Never," Phillip conceded. "But I'm not on call tonight, and I want to spend it with you. Can you meet me there?"

"Absolutely."

Phillip pushed his empty plate away. "Good. Now I've got to run. How do I look?"

"Like you spent an entire night participating in debauchery."

"Is my tie and hair straight?"

Gregory combed his fingers through the blond strands again and pretended to adjust his tie. "You're perfect."

"Love you." He kissed Gregory quickly and turned towards the door. "See you tonight."

"Yeah."

Gregory watched him from the front door, his gaze locked on Phillip as he got in the car and then headed down the street. He had seen a side of Phillip the night before that he hadn't known, and had barely suspected. For a few hours, he had let go of all the rules he loved so much, and all the restraints he put on himself. Gregory had loved it, and not just because he had enjoyed the attention of two stunningly attractive men. Nobody who saw Phillip out in the world would ever think him capable of anything except a staid and mundane existence.

But Gregory knew better. And that knowledge wrapped around Gregory's heart and tightened all the love he had already harbored for Phillip.

Gregory quietly closed the door and turned towards the

stairs. Was Jim still asleep up there, or was he biding his time? Phillip had only asked for honesty, and Gregory could give that. His heart and body was an open book to Phil, and always had been. If Phillip were there in that moment, he would see the plain desire written on Gregory's face. He still wanted Jim. A single night with Jim wasn't enough.

Taking a deep breath, he ascended the narrow stairs, straining his ears for any hints of what Jim was doing. He didn't hear anybody in the bathroom, and the bedroom was still as silent as when he slipped out the door that morning after Phillip. He nudged the door open with his foot, and was greeted by Jim's prone figure on the bed, the sheet hooked around his hips.

Gregory took a moment to stand back and simply stare at him, his mouth watering. He itched to touch him, and Phillip's words came back to him. *Have fun. Enjoy yourself.* He perched on the edge of the bed and ghosted his palm down Jim's chest, feeling the heat from his flesh but not the texture of his skin.

"I was wondering if you'd come back," Jim murmured, his voice husky with sleep.

"Well, I couldn't leave a strange man sleeping in my bed all day, could I?"

"I thought you might have left me for work."

"I have the afternoon shift today."

Jim cracked an eye open. "So, we've got a few hours?"

"I do. What about you? Don't hotshot pilots have to work like a normal person?"

"Not this hotshot pilot."

"Sounds like quite a life."

"They give me excellent benefits and other perks to make up for the fact that I could very possibly die."

Gregory grimaced. "You're like Phillip. So cavalier about...about that."

"What? Dying?"

"Yes, dying."

"It's part of the job."

"That's why I'm a librarian. Barring any freak accidents, I don't have to worry about it."

Jim took his hand, threading his fingers through Gregory's. "Would you care if I did die?"

"What sort of question is that? Of course I would."

Jim tugged him forward, so Gregory was half covering his chest, and their mouths were within inches. "So, I'm not just a one-night stand? Or a pretty face?"

"You're a pretty face, but you're definitely not a one-night stand. Unless you want to be."

The corner of Jim's mouth lifted, and his eyes sparkled. "I'm still here, aren't I? I don't stick around to exchange pleasantries after my one-night stands."

"So, you're not done corrupting me?"

"Not even close," Jim murmured, before drawing Gregory into a kiss.

Despite all appearances, Jim's mouth tasted fresh and minty, evidence that he had already gone through his morning toiletry. He even smelled a little like Phillip, like he had used the other man's soap. His lips were as firm and soft as Gregory remembered, and he responded to their easy coaxing, melting into the kiss. Their tongues danced, teasing and exploring each other's mouths.

"Why don't you get these pesky clothes off?"

Gregory moaned in protest, but only because Jim released him. He pulled his shirt off quickly, but when he noticed the

77

impatience in Jim's eyes, he grinned and slowed his pace. Jim's gaze followed Gregory's hands to his belt, and he didn't look away as Greg deliberately worked the leather free. He was accustomed to Phillip staring at him like he had never seen such a morsel, but he didn't think he'd ever be used to Jim looking at him with the same sort of desire.

He wished he knew exactly what Jim saw.

Despite his uncertainty, he didn't disrupt his striptease. Jim didn't look away as he tossed the belt aside and fingered his buttons and zipper, playing with them, but not quite undoing them. Jim licked his bottom lip, and Gregory glanced down Jim's body, noting the way the sheet was now tenting over his obvious erection.

"Are you going to tease me all morning?" Jim asked.

"I could leave."

"No, you couldn't."

"Because you won't let me, or because you don't think I have the ability to walk away?"

"Both."

"Have I mentioned this morning how modest you are?" Greg asked.

"Come here." Jim reached out before Gregory realized what he was doing, grabbing his wrist and tugging him closer to the bed. He caught Greg's zipper with the other hand and yanked it free. By the time Greg fell back to the bed, his pants were open and his cock was stiff.

"I dreamt about you last night," Jim added, his lips against Gregory's ear. "About fucking you again." He traced the outer ridge of Gregory's ear with his tongue, then sucked the lobe between his lips. "Think we could do that?"

"Oh, yes," Gregory sighed. "I think we could."

Jim reached between their bodies and wrapped his fingers around both of their cocks, squeezing the shafts together. If Gregory had any thoughts besides letting Jim fuck him, they fled in that moment. He closed his eyes, bright colors erupting behind his lids each time Jim flexed his hand. Jim's other hand worked at Gregory's pants, pushing them off his hips and down his thighs. They moved against each other, skin sliding against skin, Gregory's body coming alive everywhere he touched Jim.

Gregory sought out Jim's mouth, desperate for another taste. He was an extraordinary kisser, thorough and deliberate. Teasing, coaxing, taking what he wanted until there was nothing left to give to him. And then starting the process again. Gregory knew he must have sounded like some sort of hungry animal, whimpering and mewing for attention every time Jim paused to catch his breath. But Jim never made him wait for long. He wasn't interested in playing games, or making Gregory beg for it. He didn't seem to be interested in anything except kissing Gregory until they were both weak.

"I swear I could do this all day," Jim said against his mouth.

Gregory lifted his head and blinked. "Just this?"

Jim ran his tongue over Greg's bottom lip. "You've got the most kissable mouth."

"Thank you."

"No. Thank you."

Gregory blinked. "For what?"

"For letting me kiss it," Jim said, before claiming his lips again.

It began another round of slow, intoxicating kisses. Gregory wondered if this was Jim's evil plan—to confuse him and weaken him with his amazing mouth, until Gregory was ready to agree to any suggestion, meet any request.

Jim must have known it, because he chose that moment to speak. "Get the condoms."

Gregory responded immediately, reaching over to the side of the bed to snag the box on the table, where it had been tossed the night before. He also reached for the bottle of lube, his ass clenching as soon as he felt the cool plastic.

"I want you to ride me," Jim added, plucking the condom from Greg's fingers.

Gregory sat up and straddled Jim's thighs, wrapping his fingers around the base of Jim's shaft. His cock throbbed against Gregory's hand, and he could already feel it pushing into his body, splitting him in two. Jim unrolled the condom down his length, and it might have been Gregory's imagination, but he thought he saw Jim's fingers trembling.

"This is what I wanted from the day I met you," Jim said, his voice rasping over Gregory's skin. "I would have given anything to bring you home from the pub and get you in my bed."

"Maybe you've learned an important lesson about patience," Gregory murmured, stroking Jim with a slick hand. "Good things come to those who wait."

Jim chuckled. "I hadn't thought of it in those terms. I'm not really the waiting sort."

"Oh, I know that about you."

"You like that about me, right?"

"I like everything about you," Gregory assured him.

Jim smiled and gripped Greg's hips, pulling him forward. His cock slid between Gregory's cheeks, and everything inside of him tightened with anticipation. He began to rock, Jim's length trapped against his ass. Their mouths came together again, their tongues moving as slowly as Gregory's body. Jim moaned and lifted his hips, but otherwise did nothing to interrupt the easy rhythm. Gregory wanted Jim inside of him, but the sensation of his thick cock sliding against his ass felt too good. Gregory felt every flex of every muscle in Jim's body, every tremor, every shiver, every moan of delight and hunger.

"God, Greg..."

Gregory heard more than two simple syllables. He heard everything Jim wanted. And, fortunately, it was everything Gregory wanted too. He reached behind him to grasp Jim's cock and guided the tip to his entrance. Fusing his mouth to Jim's, he rocked back, letting Jim's cock fill him, inch by inch. When Jim was fully sheathed, Greg pushed himself to a sitting position and arched his back, savoring the pressure and sensation of Jim's magnificent cock stretching his body, forcing Gregory to accommodate him.

Greg didn't ease away from Jim's cock, even though he longed for that exquisite burn. Instead, he began grinding against Jim's body, moving his hips in slow circles. The angle and movement allowed Jim to press against his prostate. His body shuddered with pleasure each time. Jim parted his lips, and he watched Gregory with half-closed eyes. The pressure and tension built between them, increasing gradually until he thought they might both explode.

Jim finally reached up and grabbed the back of his head, forcing him into a hard kiss. As soon as Gregory's chest touched Jim's, the other man began to move, easing out of Gregory's body and then thrusting forward. Stars erupted behind Gregory's eyes, and from that moment on, he couldn't stop Jim from taking control.

Gregory had had vague thoughts about a slow fuck, appropriate for a sleepy, lazy morning, but as Jim began to move faster, those thoughts fled his mind. The sharper the rhythm, the more Gregory wanted, until he hoped Jim would flip him over and drill into him. When Jim wrapped his arms around Gregory's back, Greg thought he would do exactly that. He couldn't decide if he was disappointed or pleased that Jim used the new leverage it gave him to alter the angle so he was directly hitting Gregory's prostate again.

They moved in a sort of synchronicity that Gregory had only ever really experienced with Phillip. The thought filtered through his mind, but didn't linger long enough for Gregory to analyze it. He couldn't think of anything besides Jim's bruising tempo and the way his flesh smoldered and burned. His cock was caught between their bodies, and the friction was unbelievable. Pre-come coated his stomach, and it would be easy to turn himself over to the pleasure completely, but he didn't want to come until he felt Jim's orgasm rushing through him.

"Greg!"

The shout was more than just a sound. It was a vibration that went directly to Greg's core. He slammed into Gregory's ass with one final thrust, and then his body convulsed as he shot into the condom. Gregory briefly imagined that come coating the back of his thighs, rolling down his skin. *Next time.*

But the thought was enough to push Gregory over the edge. He buried his face against Jim's neck to muffle his own shout. Everything sizzled inside of him, his fingertips tingling, his balls aching, the hair on the back of his neck standing up.

Exhausted, he collapsed on Jim's chest, letting the other man support his weight. He didn't seem to mind.

"That was the perfect way to wake up," Jim muttered.

Gregory nodded.

"And a perfect way to work up an appetite."

"There's still breakfast downstairs."

"Thanks." His fingers moved up and down Gregory's spine in an idle caress. "Can I come by again tonight?"

Gregory didn't know how Jim could already be making plans for another round when his muscles might as well have been made of water. "Actually, Phillip informed me we have plans for tonight."

"Oh?"

"He's made reservations for us and everything." Gregory lifted his head and smiled apologetically. "I'm sorry."

"Don't apologize. What about tomorrow night?"

"If Phillip doesn't have to work, yes."

"What if he does have to work?"

"Then I'll invite you over for a quiet dinner in."

"How quiet?"

Gregory nipped at Jim's chin. "Do you just want me for the sex?"

"No, but the sex is nice."

"It is. Come over tomorrow night, and we'll see about a repeat performance."

"Fair enough."

"You're hardly argumentative at all this morning."

"I'm too tired now to be argumentative."

"So the best way to keep you sweet is to keep you sated."

"I'm always sweet."

"Aren't you hungry?"

"Yes, but I don't want to move right now."

"Me, neither." Gregory dropped his head to Jim's shoulder and let his eyes fall shut. He wasn't tired, but he did want to enjoy the warmth still suffusing his spent body. At least for a little bit longer.

Chapter Five

Gregory didn't have work emergencies like Phillip did, but once a month or so, he would find himself trapped at work. Sometimes cleaning up other people's messes, sometimes cleaning up his own. Sometimes he got caught up in a project and totally forgot there was a world outside his cool, brightly lit, sterile office. In those moments, there was nothing but the book, his instruments, and the deep satisfaction at saving said book from the ravages of time, neglect and the environment. Gregory took the time to send Phillip a quick text message, but couldn't stand to take any more attention away from his task.

He worked until grit filled his eyes, and a steady throbbing began at the base of his skull. He would have pushed himself beyond that point, but he didn't want to risk accidentally harming the book because he didn't know when to stop. By the time he locked his office and stumbled out of the library, his head was full of sawdust, and his fingers were stiff. Cleaning and restoring delicate books was a painstaking and careful process. It required an attention to detail that few people possessed or chose to use, but Gregory relished it. It could be quite tedious, but ultimately, Gregory adored anything that forced him to pay careful, thorough attention. Sometimes he suspected that was part of what attracted Phillip to him—Phillip was as anal in his own ways.

Gregory didn't feel hungry until he reached his car and saw that it was after midnight. Nothing would be open on the route to their house, though it was possible that Phillip had saved dinner for him. It was also possible that Phillip was working late himself and there would be no dinner waiting for him at all. Gregory grimaced at the thought. That meant cooking his own dinner. It would probably be easier to pass out in bed after his twelve-hour shift and worry about food in the morning.

He wasn't surprised to see Phillip's car parked in front of the house, but he was surprised to see the lights still on in the house. Had Phillip decided to wait up for him?

Gregory let himself into the house, his attention darting to the kitchen. It was empty, save for the bowl of curry waiting for him near the stove. He considered going directly upstairs, but his stomach had other ideas, and he turned towards the kitchen instead. He popped it in the microwave for a few moments and took a cold beer out of the fridge, his mouth watering for the crisp liquid.

He had the bottle half drained and was about to take a bite of his curry when he heard what sounded like a shout coming from upstairs. Not a shout of distress, though. Curious, he abandoned his plans for dinner and made his way to the second floor, straining his ears for any other sounds. By the time he reached the landing, he was certain that it wasn't Phillip he heard. Jim was there too.

Gregory paused outside the partially closed bedroom door, unsure if he wanted to open it and find out exactly what was going on. He and Phillip had talked several times about where Jim fit in their life, and what reasonable expectations were for both of them. They had agreed that either one of them could have sex with Jim without prior permission, but Phillip had never seemed interested in fucking Jim when Gregory wasn't present. Jim had even made an off-hand reference to it, asking

85

if Phillip had something against him. Gregory had denied that as a possibility, though sometimes the same thought crossed his mind.

Ultimately, curiosity prompted him to nudge the door open and peer into the dim bedroom. Phillip straddled Jim's thighs, his hands free to explore Jim's body. Jim had his hands stretched above his head, and for a moment, Gregory thought Phillip had cuffed him to the bed. But there was no glint of metal in the low light, and Gregory realized he was just gripping the bed. Gregory couldn't see Phillip's face, but he imagined it easily enough. His brow would be furrowed with concentration, and his eyes would be half-closed.

He did, however, see Jim's face. Jim seemed to be enthralled, like he had never expected to be in that particular position with that particular man, but now he knew he didn't want to be anywhere else. Phillip's body blocked Jim's cock from Gregory's view, but Greg didn't need to see it. His mouth watered at the thought of Jim's thick, erect cock, and his groin tightened as he imagined fitting his mouth around both Jim and Phil's heads.

Gregory could push the door open and reveal himself. Both men would welcome him into the bed. They'd cover him with their mouths and their hands. They'd surround him and overwhelm his senses. They'd take turns making him scream and beg for more. They'd make him forget there was a world outside their bedroom. There wasn't anything better in Gregory's opinion, but he didn't want that right then. They'd welcome him, but he didn't want to interrupt them. He wanted to see what would happen between them.

Gregory wanted Jim to like Phillip. More than that, he wanted Jim to be as impressed with Phillip as Gregory was. He wanted Jim to see everything that Gregory saw. He wanted Jim to see all the passion and desire that Phillip harbored, hidden beneath the surface. He didn't quite know why this was so important to him, but he couldn't think of anything he wanted more in that moment.

Phillip moved down Jim's body, dragging his palms over the other man's firm chest. Once again, Greg was struck by the contrast between them. They were so different; it seemed impossible for Gregory to be so attracted to both of them. But in many ways, they were so alike that Gregory didn't stand a chance against either of them.

Watching Phillip touch and kiss another man the way he always touched Gregory should have been awkward, but it was only fascinating. Now he could see that Phil used his entire body when he made love to another person, every muscle engaged in the act. He moved further down Jim's body, bending at the waist to lick and nip at his chest and stomach. Jim writhed beneath Phil's talented mouth, his breath catching as Phillip finally reached his cock.

Phillip licked Jim's shaft from the base to the tip over and over. Each long lick was thorough, and Gregory's pants seemed to get tighter every time Phillip moved up Jim's cock. It soon became obvious to Gregory that the only way he'd relieve himself from the pain was to unzip his pants, but he didn't want to risk making any noise and distracting Phillip. So he pulled at his pants and shifted his weight, trying to decrease his discomfort even as Jim began to moan and move his hips.

Phillip treated the man beneath him like an ice cream cone. Occasionally, he paused from the licking to wrap his lips around the tip and suck the pre-come from the skin. Each time Phil applied a bit of suction to the sensitive flesh, Jim jerked and tried to push his cock further into Phillip's mouth. Phillip was having none of it, though. Gregory didn't think Phil wanted to torment Jim, but regardless of his ultimate motive, that's exactly what he was doing. Gregory saw it on Jim's face, heard it with every moan, even smelled it.

Jim put his feet against the bed and bent his knees, spreading his legs wider for Phillip. Phil cupped Jim's balls, tugging with firm fingers with every swipe of his tongue. Jim's moans were loud enough to hide Gregory's quickening breaths, and he didn't know if he wanted to trade places with Phil or Jim. Phil's mouth was amazing and his patience exquisite—he could continue like that all night without a problem. But Jim's cock was gorgeous, and it deserved that sort of attention. It deserved more than that sort of attention.

Phillip slid his hand up Jim's body, his fingers seeking out his lips. Jim obediently parted his lips and sucked Phillip's fingers into his mouth. His cheeks hollowed as he wet Phil's skin, and he moaned in protest when Phil pulled his hand away. His disappointment was short lived, because Phil slid his newly wet fingers between Jim's legs, seeking out his tight hole.

"God, Phil. You're going to..." The words were caught in a shout, and Gregory knew exactly what Phillip had done. He always knew how to massage the prostate, working his fingers until words and thought, and even breath, was impossible.

Phillip continued his slow, patient assault. Gregory knew that Jim was very greedy for contact. If Phillip had told him that he could drive any man to distraction with nothing more than his tongue and two fingers, Jim probably would have scoffed. He would have demanded Phillip swallow him down completely. He would have insisted he pound into Phillip's ass. Jim wasn't shy.

But Phillip wasn't the type to be bullied.

He didn't pump his wrist or create any sort of friction between his fingers and Jim's ass. But Jim never stopped moving, never stopped reacting. He jerked. He thrust against Phil's hand. He arched his back. He moaned and shouted Phil's name and cried out for more. Phillip's fingers remained buried in Jim's channel, and his tongue continued in slow and deliberate strokes.

"Phil..." Jim's voice was low, and it vibrated through Gregory's body. He felt it more than he heard it. He might have been begging. Pleading. Praying. It was impossible to tell, but it made Gregory ache.

Phillip grunted, as if he felt the pleasure building beneath Jim's skin. And then Jim erupted, shouting as his come coated Phillip's lips and chin. Phillip stuck his tongue out, catching as much of the streaming liquid as he could before crawling up Jim's body. Jim gripped the side of Phil's head, his palms over Phil's ears, and began to lick the come from his face. Once his cheek and chin was cleaned, he focused on Phil's lips, claiming his mouth in a long, searching kiss.

"My God...no wonder Gregory loves you so much."

Phillip smiled and dropped his head to Jim's shoulder. "I aim to please."

Gregory took a small step back. He knew he should go in, but he wanted to see what would happen next.

"Is he going to be home soon?"

"Should be. He usually isn't out much later than this."

"You use that trick on him?"

"Sure."

"Will you show me how you do it?"

Phillip smiled. "It's not that difficult. You just have to be patient."

Jim grimaced. "Yeah, not really my strong suit."

"So Greg tells me."

"I'm glad I came over tonight. You don't mind when I drop in, do you?"

Phillip rolled off Jim's chest and settled on his back, staring up at the ceiling. "No. Though you were lucky I was home. I'm usually not at that hour."

"You ever going to be able to slow down?"

"When I retire, I suppose."

"You're not going to do that for years, though."

"No. But this is what I always wanted."

"I know what you mean. My job isn't exactly the safest one around, and it's difficult to have any sort of social life. But Gregory...he makes it easier."

"That's because I give him all sorts of spare time." Phillip sighed. "I don't know why he puts up with it."

"Because he loves you."

"Yeah. Sometimes I think he deserves better, though."

"I'm sure he doesn't think so. There's something I don't understand, though. I mean, I wouldn't be interested in sharing Greg with anybody, if I were in your shoes..."

"So, you're wondering why I didn't make you leave him alone?"

"Yeah."

"I like you. You like him. He likes you. God knows he doesn't deserve to spend his nights alone. And besides, I..." Phillip paused, as if rethinking the words he was about to utter.

"You what?"

"Nothing."

Jim turned on his side, resting his head on his palm. "I hope you don't plan on getting rid of me any time soon, because I don't plan on going anywhere."

"I doubt Gregory would let you go anywhere. He seems content to have you around."

That had been true, but now Gregory wasn't so sure. Something about Phillip's explanation didn't sit right with him. Until he could put his finger on what, he didn't feel like he'd be fit company for either of them. He backed further from the door and quietly descended the stairs.

"So, what exactly are you waiting for?" Phillip asked from the bottom of the stairs.

Gregory looked up from the book he was reading, then glanced at the clock above the television. Ten after two.

"I'm sorry. I didn't realize it was so late."

"I can't believe you chose a book over us."

Gregory smiled and put his marker between the pages. "It was a very engrossing book."

"More engrossing than two hard pricks?"

"You knew I was a book geek when we met."

Phillip stepped into the living room, revealing the fact that he was still naked. At the first glimpse of him, Gregory wanted to lick the line of his hip. "Why don't you come upstairs now?"

Gregory took Phil's offered hand and stood. "Is Jim staying all night?"

"Yeah. Unless you want him to go home, but if so, you're the one who's going to have to wake him up."

"No, that's fine."

Phillip tugged at his hand. "What's wrong?"

"Why do you think there's something wrong?"

"I can see it in your eyes. Plus, you chose a book over the two of us." Phillip frowned. "You're not angry because we were...upstairs together, are you?"

"What? No. No, not at all." Gregory licked his lips. There was no way Phillip was going to let him claim everything was great. Honesty. He had promised honesty. "I was thinking...I was wondering why we're doing this."

"Doing what?"

"Jim."

"Aren't you having fun?"

"Well, sure. But it's not really a matter of having fun, is it? It's...he's here more and more. Sleeping over more and more."

"And you don't like that?"

"No, that's not what I'm saying." He pulled Phillip over to the couch and sat down. He wanted to curl up against Phil's body, but if he did that, he would forget all about talking. "I don't understand why you're so...willing to let another person into our home and our bed. This isn't like you, Phil. And I was so caught up in the novelty of it all that I didn't really think about it. But I'm thinking about it now, and I need to know what's going on."

Now it was Phillip's turn to hesitate. Gregory kept a hold of his hand, a firm reminder that he wasn't going to let this go. Not until he had an answer.

"Do you remember last month when that civilian got hurt?"

"Yeah."

"I almost...I almost didn't come home that night. He almost ran me over too. And in that split second as I rolled out of the way of the tires, I thought about you. What it would mean if I never came home again. And I...I didn't want to do that to you. I didn't want to leave you alone. And you met Jim..."

"What are you saying? That you want Jim to be your fill-in?"

"Not quite. I thought...you deserve to be with somebody who you can count on. That maybe..."

"That maybe I'd what? Realize I've fallen in love with Jim?"

"Yeah."

"You do realize that the safe replacement you chose for me is a pilot who tests prototypes, right? Every time he leaves for work, he has the chance of plummeting to the ground in a horrible, fiery death."

Phillip frowned and looked away. "Well, I would have preferred a nice, safe accountant, but you appear to have a thing for the dangerous types."

Gregory's heart twisted. "Phil...I don't want a replacement. I want you. I'm in love with you. You're my best friend."

"I could die tomorrow."

"So could I. You must have known this wasn't going to work. Unless...is this your way of breaking up with me?"

"No!" Phillip cupped the back of his neck and pulled Gregory forward, until their brows touched. "You're the best thing in my life. That's why I couldn't stand the thought of...letting you down like that. Of hurting you like that."

"That's sweet, Phil. Misguided and self-centered, but sweet. But you're not going to be able to get rid of me. I know that your job is dangerous. I came to terms with that a long time ago. Besides, this isn't London, is it? It's pretty quiet here. You were just shaken up and not thinking clearly."

"So you'll forgive me for being an idiot?"

"Every time."

"I think I better go home," Jim said from the hallway.

Gregory and Phillip jumped apart, both of them startled by Jim's unusually soft voice.

"You don't have to go home," Gregory protested.

"No, I think I do."

Greg stood. "We were about to go upstairs."

"You should still go upstairs. But I've got an early day tomorrow, so..."

He still sounded too quiet. Subdued. Gregory's heart felt heavy. Jim didn't look like a happy man.

"I really wish you would stay. We both do, don't we, Phil?"

Phillip was suddenly at his side, his hand on Gregory's shoulder. "Yeah. At least get some sleep. It's already pretty late."

"No. I'll call you."

Gregory had heard that before. It sounded like a brush-off, and it usually was. He must have overheard the conversation with Phillip. Was he leaving before they had the chance to send him away? But if that were the case, why would he insist on going even after they both asked him to stay?

"Okay. Do you want me to give you a lift home?"

"I'll walk. It's fine, Greg."

"Jim..."

Phillip tightened his grip on Gregory's shoulder, stopping him from taking a step forward. Greg tried to shrug him away, but Phil merely muttered, "Let him go."

Jim nodded at them both then shrugged on his jacket and let himself out the door.

"I don't understand..."

"He thinks we were using him," Phillip said.

"But we weren't. I wasn't. I didn't want him to go."

"Do you want this to be a more permanent relationship?"

Gregory looked from Phil to the closed door and back again. "I...I don't know. Do you?"

"I don't know. Maybe we should sleep on it."

Gregory was scared if they let Jim go in that moment, they would never see him again. But he didn't know what to say. Didn't know what to do. He had never been in this sort of situation, and the realization that he wanted both men in his life was too hard to accept fully. A part of him had always thought their time with Jim would be brief—just a fling. Casual.

But if it was casual, watching Jim walk out wouldn't be so hard.

Chapter Six

Every time Gregory heard a plane overhead, he'd look up. Sometimes it was a jet, lost in the sky and almost impossible to see. Sometimes it was much closer, clearly bound for the air force base. He always imagined Jim was in the cockpit, and that thought hurt, but made him feel a little better too. Like they were still connected, even though Jim hadn't called. Gregory contacted him once, but Jim had been distant and distracted. Gregory took the hint.

It felt like they had only been on a small detour, and now everything was right again. Phillip still came and went at all hours, but Gregory made sure they always had a few hours together every day. He had taken more hours at the library and had been assigned a massive project that could take an entire year, so he had plenty to occupy his time and his thoughts. The fact of the matter was, he didn't need Jim. Jim had been a diversion—and a fun one at that—but not necessary.

Whenever that thought entered Gregory's head, he rejected it. Was anybody really necessary? Did he *need* Phillip? No, he would survive without him. It wouldn't be pleasant. He wouldn't want to do it. But he could live. What did it mean to need another human being?

That was the question Jim had unwittingly planted in his mind.

What did it mean to need somebody with golden hair and golden skin? What did it mean to need a mischievous smile and flirting hazel eyes? Did it mean living with a strong sense of disappointment when Jim didn't knock on his door? Did it mean he needed somebody with blond hair and blue eyes less? Did needing somebody automatically mean loving somebody? Could there really be a difference between the two?

If Phillip grappled with the same questions, he didn't let on. Neither one of them talked about Jim, though Gregory was sure Phillip knew that living without the other man in their lives was painful. It didn't make sense, but it was always between them. This empty space that hadn't been there before. This vacuum where there should be teasing, and kissing, and joking, and laughing. But at the same time, those things weren't missing from their lives.

Everything was normal.

Except everything was different.

A part of Gregory was waiting for Phillip to fix everything. Phillip was good at that. But as the days went by, and their holding pattern continued, Gregory realized it would be up to him. He'd have to take the first step.

"Do you miss Jim?" Gregory asked one night over soup.

"Yeah."

"Not because you thought he would make a good substitute?"

"No. I miss gardening with him. And eating with him." Phillip slurped at his soup. "I miss the way he looked at you, and I always knew exactly what he was thinking."

"I miss him too. I think...I should go talk to him."

"You should."

"You're not going to volunteer to go with me?"

"Do you want me to?"

Gregory stirred his soup. "I don't know. A unified front might be better. But I don't know."

"I think you should go talk to him. I think it would mean more to him."

"When?"

"There's no time like the present."

Gregory didn't even finish his soup. He kissed Phillip goodbye then grabbed his keys and went out the door. On the short drive over, he tried to plot out what he would say. But he wasn't sure what Jim wanted to hear from them. There was a very good chance that Jim had left because he wanted to leave. He was done with them, and there'd be nothing Greg could say or do to change his mind.

But he wouldn't let that thought dissuade him. He didn't allow himself to hesitate when he reached Jim's flat, though it would have been much easier to sit in the car and continue to fret and worry over what he needed to say. By the time he reached the door, he wished that Phillip had accompanied him. A unified front would be better, he was suddenly sure of it.

The slight widening of Jim's eyes betrayed his surprise at Gregory's appearance. But his voice was neutral when he spoke.

"Gregory. Come in."

"Thanks."

"What can I do for you?"

Gregory looked around the room, a lump forming in his chest. "You can tell me why your flat is full of boxes."

"Moving."

"Where? I thought you said you were going to be in Cambridge for awhile?"

"I got the chance to work in the States again. I thought it was a good opportunity."

"Oh. Well. Congratulations."

"Thanks. Do you want to sit down? Can I get you something to drink? Beer? I still don't know how to make proper tea."

"No, I'm fine. Thank you." Gregory swallowed. "So, when are you set to go?"

"The end of the week."

"You weren't...going to say goodbye?"

"I thought I already had."

"Oh. I guess...in that case I should probably go. Don't want to waste your time. It was good seeing you. Have a safe trip."

Gregory turned towards the door, but he was stopped by a simple request. "Wait, Greg."

"Yeah?"

"I thought this would be easier. For all of us."

"Which part? Moving to the States? Not speaking to us anymore?"

"All of it."

The flat wasn't large, but it felt like they were separated by an impossible chasm. Gregory didn't dare take a step forward to close the distance. He wasn't sure he knew this man—the one who would run away from a problem instead of tackling it head on.

"Well, it's not easier for me. I've missed you, and I don't even know what I've done to offend you."

"I overheard the discussion you and Phil had."

"I figured as much."

"I thought I would get out with my pride intact."

Gregory shook his head. "I don't know what you think we were going to do to your pride."

"I don't want to be somebody's substitute. I don't want you to spend time with me just because Phillip is busy. I knew that I would never have you all to myself, and I thought I could live with that. I know I could live with that. But I don't want to be your back-up cock. You know, break glass in case of emergency."

"I...I never thought of you like that, Jim. I guess you don't have to believe me. I'd even understand if you didn't. But I never, ever thought of you like that."

"Phillip did."

"I think Phillip took a small break from reality for a few weeks, but he's better now. He likes you because he likes you, not because he..." Now Gregory did take a step forward, watching to make sure Jim didn't try to move away from him. "He made a mistake. A big one. And he's sorry."

Jim shook his head. "You've got a good thing with Phillip. You don't need me being a third wheel."

"Maybe I do need you to be a third wheel. Maybe we'd work better as a tricycle than a bicycle."

Jim's lips twitched. "A tricycle?"

"Okay, it was a stupid metaphor. But can you name another vehicle with a third wheel?"

"No. Which proves my point."

"It proves my point. Things with three wheels are rare, but they do exist. Anyway, all I know is I've missed you. I've missed talking to you. I've missed kissing you. I've missed sharing a pint with you. We were friends first, and I miss that. I also miss falling asleep with you. And eating breakfast with you. I even miss waiting for you to come home at night because at least I know you are coming home and you haven't had some horrible, bloody accident."

"You think about the last thing a lot, don't you?"

"All the time. Your job terrifies me."

"You still need to come up in a plane with me. Let me show you how easy and safe it is to fly."

"You mean, how it feels to fall in controlled circumstances."

"That too."

"I can't now. You're leaving at the end of the week, and I haven't got any time off."

"I can tell you're really sad that you're missing your chance to fly."

Gregory snorted. "The hell of it is, Jim, I really am. I hope you find what you're looking for in the States."

Jim sighed and slid his fingers in his pockets, pulling his jeans tight across his crotch. Gregory regretted not joining Jim and Phillip in bed that final night, more than he had ever regretted anything else. Maybe if he had, the whole night would have gone differently, and they wouldn't be saying their farewells now.

"I don't think I will."

"Why not?"

"I've already found what I'm looking for here in Cambridge. And the hell of it is, I don't want to leave now."

"You don't have to, do you?"

"It's my job, Greg."

"A job. Not a life-sentence or a punishment." Gregory half-turned towards the door. He was disappointed, but at least he had tried. And he didn't have to be alone at home. At least Phillip would understand. "But a job you love. I know. Just take care of yourself, okay?"

"Gregory..."

Gregory didn't let Jim stop him again. His heart felt like it was breaking, and he didn't see any reason to prolong this particular brand of torment. Jim was leaving. He wanted a real relationship, and he deserved that much. Could things really be equal between the three of them? Gregory thought so, but he didn't know for sure.

He pulled the door open, only to have it immediately slam shut again. Jim's hand was above his head, holding it closed, and Gregory was forced to turn around to face him.

"You don't just want me to scratch an itch when Phil isn't home?"

"No."

"You'll go flying with me?"

"I...yes."

"You're not saying that to placate the crazy person?"

Jim's mouth was so close now, it was a little hard to concentrate. But Gregory focused on the question instead of how much he wanted a kiss. "No."

Jim's nostrils flared as he inhaled Gregory's scent. "Do you mind if I come home with you?"

"Will you stay? It'll be too hard to go through this goodbye again."

"I'll stay."

"That's all I needed to hear." Gregory took Jim's hand, their fingers entwining. "Come on. Phil is waiting for us."

"Does Phil do that thing with his fingers a lot?"

"Only when he really wants to make you crazy. Or prove a point."

Jim opened the door without releasing Gregory. "He was trying to prove a point."

"He'll also do it if you ask nicely."

Jim grinned. "Good to know. I'll even say please."

"Before or during?"

"Both."

Jim locked the door behind them, and for the first time since Jim left their house, the empty spaces began to fill.

Phillip greeted Jim with a kiss. The sort of kiss reserved for a reunion after a long absence. He pushed Jim back against the wall, fisting his shirt, his tongue demanding entry into Jim's mouth. It was the sort of kiss that meant business. The sort of kiss that didn't leave any room for ambiguity. Gregory watched, his cock hardening, as Jim responded, first with surprise, and then with obvious hunger.

"I wasn't sure if Gregory would bring you home," Phillip said, when he finally lifted his head.

"He's very convincing."

Phillip glanced over to Greg, who responded with a half-smile. "I used my words, not my mouth."

"But you could use your mouth now, if you want," Jim informed him.

"I planned on it."

Phillip pulled Jim towards the stairs. "Come on, let's go up to the bedroom."

"I guess Gregory was telling the truth. You did miss me."

"I did."

Gregory followed them up the stairs, the back of his neck and the bottoms of his feet tingling. He wasn't nervous, but he was more excited than the first time they had brought Jim up to their room. This was different. They had a different understanding. Because Jim wasn't going to be merely a guest in their bed, he was going to be a part of their lives.

As soon as they stepped into the bedroom, Phillip diverted his attention from Jim to focus on Gregory. He gently pushed Greg towards the bed, placing him at the center of attention. His balls tightened as both men looked at him with hunger in their eyes, and the tingling he experienced spread through his whole body. Like they were transmitting their desire to him, to his blood and bones. He pulled his shirt over his head before either of them spoke, and then toed off his shoes.

Jim reached for Greg first, pulling his belt free before unzipping his pants. Gregory watched Jim's hands, but a soft sigh—a sound that could have been his name—forced Gregory to look up. Jim's gaze caught and held his attention, his eyes that curious, intense hazel. He sought Gregory's face, and Greg returned his stare, unblinking. Everything he had said to Jim that night had been true. If Jim still doubted him, Gregory hoped he saw the sincerity in his eyes.

Whatever Jim saw there, it must have been what he was searching for. He cupped the back of Gregory's head, and then their mouths met. Greg couldn't know for sure, but he thought this kiss perfectly mirrored the one Phillip had given Jim. It was demanding and promising at the same time, searching and giving. It was tinged with more than a little relief, and Gregory responded in kind, wrapping his arms around Jim's solid body to press their chests together.

Always aware of Phillip, he listened as the other man undressed, the whisper of his clothes falling to the floor penetrating the growing fog around Gregory's mind. He heard

Phillip cross the room, opening and closing the bedside table, and then settling on the bed behind Greg. His hands were welcome as they moved down Gregory's spine, his thumbs massaging the tension out of Greg's muscles.

"Have you ever been fucked by two cocks at the same time?" Jim asked without lifting his head.

"You don't mean sucking one of those cocks, right?"

"Right."

Gregory throat tightened. He had occasionally thought about how it would feel to be double penetrated, but he never thought to ask, and he never believed either Phillip or Jim would suggest it. The thought of feeling both men at the same time, in the same way, made his knees feel watery.

"No, I've never done that."

"Do you want to?"

Gregory hesitated and looked over his shoulder. Phillip didn't even blink. "He does."

"I spent every day vowing to walk away from you," Jim murmured, "and every night dreaming about fucking you again."

The corners of his mouth pricked as Gregory thought about some of his own dreams. The one he remembered with the most clarity was getting on his knees between the two men and taking turns licking and sucking their cocks. His palms felt clammy and his fingers eager as he tore at Jim's clothes, struggling to remove his shirt and his pants. Instead of helping him, Jim claimed his lips again. Gregory didn't allow himself to be distracted by the caress, and before they broke apart, he had Jim's pants around his ankles and his shirt hanging open.

Gregory fisted Jim's cock, glad to feel its weight and warmth against his palm again. The desire to use his mouth on

Jim returned, amplified, and Gregory moaned in mingled frustration and hunger, trying to break away from both Jim and Phillip, though neither seemed interested in letting him move.

"What do you want?" Jim asked, his lips against Gregory's.

"To suck you. Both of you."

Jim smiled. "Well, I guess that can be arranged."

Phillip stood as Jim stepped back, and for a moment, Gregory was trapped between their chests. He had a chance to register the differences in how they felt—Jim had more hair on his chest, the texture of Phillip's skin was more familiar—and then a hand on his shoulder pushed him down to the floor.

Gregory sighed as his mouth became level with both cocks. A clear drop of pre-come was already gathering on Jim's slit, and his tongue darted out to collect the fluid. He took time to study Jim's cock, becoming acquainted once again with its thickness and length, the way it curved upward slightly, and the fact that he was cut.

He gripped both Jim and Phillip, holding their cocks in place as he tilted his head to wrap his lips around Jim's cock. His tongue dipped into the slit, and he let his teeth scrape against the head in the lightest of caresses. He could have continued like that all night, but he felt the tip of Phillip's head push against the corner of his mouth, demanding attention. Gregory refocused immediately, his mouth closing over Phillip's velvety crown.

Gregory split his attention between them, moving back and forth, marking each difference and each similarity. Their tastes mingled on his tongue—pre-come, and sweat, and the natural flavor of their skin. Everything was salty and somehow sweet, and Gregory's head spun. Finally, he tired of taking them one at a time, and he relaxed his jaw, opening his mouth as wide as he could before guiding both cocks past his lips.

Both Jim and Phillip moaned, and Gregory's cock jerked. He wished he had another hand so he could stroke himself as he sucked on their heads, but he needed both hands to hold them in place. He closed his eyes as his lips stretched around their shafts, and their crowns rubbed against each other and his tongue. Phillip put a hand in his hair, his fingers tight against Gregory's scalp, and Jim began to caress his jaw and his cheek. He tried to imagine would it would feel like to have both cocks in his ass, but he couldn't quite comprehend it. He had a feeling he wouldn't be able to until he experienced it.

"God, Gregory..."

"Don't stop, Greg..."

Their accents and their voices mingled, until Gregory couldn't tell who was talking to him. He only heard words of encouragement, and each syllable went directly to his groin. His cock leaked and his balls ached, and his whole body cried out to be touched, but he had to settle for the way their words felt and the pressure and texture of their cocks in his mouth.

Jim broke first. "Greg...I can't take any more..."

He pulled away and Gregory sat back on his heels, his mouth still watering for more. He eyed Phillip's cock, the back of his throat itching at the thought of swallowing his length and holding him in his throat. But Phillip stepped out of reach too.

"Let's get this ass ready."

They both pulled Gregory to his feet, and he stretched out on the bed on his stomach, bracing himself on his elbows. Phillip stood in front of him, his cock glistening, waiting to find its place between Gregory's lips again. He heard Jim behind him, but he expected to feel slick fingers or a hot tongue against his flushed skin. He did not expect to feel the blunt head of Jim's cock, pushing for entry.

Gregory opened his mouth to ask what Jim was doing, but

Phillip took advantage of his parted lips to slide his cock against Gregory's tongue. Jim moved at the same time, easing his length into Gregory's tight hole. Once again, Gregory wished he could reach his shaft to stroke it. The pressure was allowed to build beneath his skin, and he pushed his hips against the mattress, trying to find some friction that way.

Jim began slow, moaning and murmuring Gregory's name. He placed his hand on the top of Greg's head and pushed forward, guiding him down Phil's cock. Each time he moved his hips, he pushed on Gregory's head, until Gregory felt like he was continuously filled. Either Jim's cock was fully sheathed in his ass, or Phil's head was twitching against the back of Gregory's throat.

He had forgotten how good it felt when Jim fucked him. His cock was a bit thicker than Phillip's, and it stretched him differently. Jim moved differently, too, finding a rhythm that was unique to him. Greg thought about how close he came to losing this, and how much he would have missed being caught between the two of them, his body at their mercy.

Phillip leaned forward, and they both thrust into Gregory at the same time as their mouths came together. Gregory didn't see them kiss, but he heard them, and the small moans they made in the back of their throats. He felt them both vibrating, each tremor echoed in Gregory's flesh. Their kiss sent an entirely new bolt of desire through Gregory, and he realized he wanted to watch them again. He wanted to take a seat away from the bed and stroke himself slowly as they kissed and caressed and fucked each other. And then he wanted to lick the come from their bodies, off their abs and asses and thighs and balls.

When their kiss broke, Jim bent at the waist, and Gregory felt his hot mouth on the back of his shoulder. His lips and tongue were gentle, in complete contrast to his tight hands and

108

his driving hips. He nibbled on Gregory's skin, soothed the marks with his tongue, skimmed his lips over the back of Gregory's neck, let his hot breath blow across Gregory's hair.

"Do you think he's ready for both of us?" Phillip asked.

Gregory's ass clenched at the question. Jim groaned. "Yes, I think he is."

Phillip pulled away from Gregory and reached for the box of condoms. Jim didn't stop moving as Phillip unrolled the latex down his length. Jim slammed forward into Gregory's ass again and again, grunting each time Gregory's tightened around him. Once Phil had the condom on, he slicked his cock with lube, running his palm up and down his shaft, almost leisurely, his heavy eyes trained on Jim.

"Don't just stand there," Jim said, "he's waiting for you."

"How do you want to do this?" Phil asked.

"You lay down."

Gregory wanted to collapse on the bed by the time Jim pulled out of him, but he was still quivering and aching to be filled again. Phillip stretched out beside him on the mattress, and then pulled Gregory onto his body, their slick chests pressed together. Their mouths met, and Gregory practically melted against Phillip's familiar form, welcoming his warm, slick skin. Phil's cock nudged his stretched hole, and it was a simple matter of rocking backwards, bearing down until Phillip filled him completely.

"Like that," Jim murmured. "That's right."

Gregory felt the mattress shift beneath them as Jim joined them on the bed. Then Jim pressed against the back of his thighs, his flesh hot and taut. Gregory caught his breath, everything inside his body tense and frozen in place.

"Relax." Phillip ran his fingers over his damp brow. "Relax,

Greg. You're too tense."

Gregory nodded because he couldn't speak. He was too tense, and his throat was tight, and his tongue was dry. And Jim's cock was right there, ready to slide against Phil's length and right into Gregory's passage. Greg lifted his head, his attention locked on Phil's blue eyes. He couldn't help but smile a little, and Phillip returned his grin.

"Just stay relaxed..."

Gregory nodded.

"Stop us if it's too much."

Gregory nodded again. And then Jim's mouth was at his ear. "Don't let me hurt you."

"I won't. You won't. It's fine."

Greg had no doubt he would scream by the time Jim entered him, but he was still completely unprepared for how it would feel and how he would react. At first, as the tip of Jim's cock pushed into him, he wanted to resist. He couldn't take both of them at once. It was foolish to think so. He should stop them, and let Phillip fuck him while he sucked Jim off. But he didn't stop Jim, and then Jim pushed forward another inch. And another. Gregory thought he was being split into two pieces. There was an unfamiliar pain as his body tried to adjust to the new intrusion, and then the pain moved on to something else.

Something Gregory had never experienced before.

Something he had no name for.

Whatever he was feeling, he saw it reflected in Phillip's eyes. And heard it in Jim's voice as he shouted. Whatever it was, he wasn't feeling it alone. The fact that both Phillip and Jim felt it only intensified this alien sensation, until his cells were vibrating and his body was in danger of flying apart. He hadn't felt this close to anybody in his life, and now he felt like he was a part of not one, but two men. And they were a part of him.

Somebody needed to move. It was Jim who ultimately broke first, dragging his cock along Phil's as he slid out, and then gently pushed forward. Everything was gentle at first. Jim was barely moving, yet Gregory felt like Jim was pounding into him. Phillip clutched at him, his fingers digging into Gregory's flesh hard enough to leave bruises. Gregory's cock was trapped, still aching for contact, still throbbing against his stomach.

After several beats, Jim began to move faster. That's when Gregory lost it, screaming their names. They were both shouting too. The pressure and heat inside his body was exquisite, and he imagined the added friction of their cocks sliding against one another was enough to drive both Phillip and Jim crazy. He didn't know how long he could tolerate it, and he didn't know if he ever wanted it to end.

Jim directed the tempo, and Phillip remained still beneath him, his cock remaining buried in Gregory's ass. Phil wasn't a particularly vocal lover, but even he couldn't keep his shouts and moans suppressed. Occasionally, words would fall from their lips. Gregory cursing and promising devotion, Phillip shouting to God, and Jim offering endless encouragement, begging Gregory not to make him stop.

Gregory wouldn't make him stop, but they couldn't continue like that. Not indefinitely. There was too much pleasure and need and desire and friction. Jim rested his forehead against Gregory's shoulder, his soft words traveling to Greg's ear.

"Not going to last..."

"I know..."

"So close...Greg...God..."

"Jim..."

Gregory didn't know who came first, if it was Phillip or Jim. They might have come at the same time. All he knew was that he felt both cocks jerk against his walls, felt both men's moans of satisfaction, felt their muscles tense and convulse, felt that moment of tension when everything was too hard, and that sweet breath of relief.

"Please...please...please..." Gregory panted, so close to the edge, but still not quite capable of losing complete control.

Phillip gripped his cock, squeezing it tightly, almost to the point of pain. They were both buried in his ass still, the pressure unbelievable. Gregory began rocking his hips, eliciting another moan from them as he fucked himself on their semi-erect cocks. Jim's chest slid against his back, the damp hair tickling his skin. And then he felt Jim's lips on the nape of his neck. A simple, soft kiss. It sent a bolt of electricity directly down his spine and then everything exploded.

He stilled, his cock shooting all over Phil's hand and stomach, his ass clenching around their lengths. He closed his eyes and saw blue and green and gold and white. He saw himself entwined between their bodies, like that's where he fit, and he wouldn't fit anywhere else.

Gregory lost all strength in his arms and fell forward, collapsing on top of Phillip. Jim eased away, disposing of his condom before laying down beside them. Greg didn't think his breathing would ever return to normal, and his heart still pounded in his ears.

"I've never...even thought anything like that was possible," Jim murmured. "You okay, Greg?"

Gregory nodded without lifting his head.

"I think we might have broken him."

"I think that's probably what he wanted."

Gregory smiled. Or thought about smiling. He didn't have high hopes about regaining the full use of his muscles any time soon.

"I think I need to rest for a few minutes," Jim added.

"Yes, that sounds good."

Gregory gathered up what remained of his strength. "Don't leave. Phil, don't let him leave."

"I won't," Jim promised. "I'm not going anywhere."

"Good. Can't be without you."

"Nobody's going anywhere," Phil assured him.

Gregory rested his cheek on Phil's shoulder and closed his eyes, satisfied that when he opened them again, Jim would still be there.

Chapter Seven

Gregory took one look at the small airplane and spun on his heel, intent on returning to the hangar. Jim caught him by the arm, though, and refused to let him take another step.

"Where do you think you're going?"

"I'm not getting in that thing."

"Why not?"

"It's small."

Jim shook his head. "It's perfectly safe."

"It looks like it'll break apart as soon as you take off."

"It won't. I've taken that up in the air two or three dozen times."

Gregory tried to pull his arm away. "If God intended for us to fly, he would have given us wings."

"He didn't need to give us wings. He gave us the intelligence to build an airplane, and he gave the world somebody like me to fly it."

Greg swallowed. "Jim, I don't want to."

"I know you're scared. But if you're going to conquer your fears, you've got to face them. Head on."

"Where did you hear that crap?"

"That's what Phillip told you this morning when you were

cowering in the bathroom. You agreed with him."

"Oh. I didn't think you overheard that."

"Well, I did. Now come on."

Gregory allowed himself to be dragged back towards the plane. He knew he promised. He knew he agreed with Phillip, that it was important for him to face this fear. He knew that he would never travel the world and visit all the cities he longed to visit if he couldn't even get on a bloody airplane. But he also knew he didn't want to die, and his chances of dying increased exponentially the further away he got from the ground.

"It's going to be a short flight," Jim promised him. "We'll be landing again before you know it."

It took all of Gregory's courage to climb into the plane, and when he saw how cramped the space was, he tried to turn around again. But Jim wouldn't let him.

"You're going to be fine, I promise."

"I'm really scared."

"I know. But you're a brave guy, Greg. Here, let's get you buckled in."

Gregory's hands were shaking too badly for him to secure the belt, but Jim took over without a word and did it for him. The chair was narrow and uncomfortable, and the windshield seemed much too small. How could Jim see everything he needed to see? There was a dizzying array of buttons and monitors on the dashboard, and it seemed impossible for any one person to know what it all meant. Even somebody as smart as Jim.

"We won't stay up for long, right?"

"Nope. Just a quick little jaunt."

"And you won't do any fancy tricks? No loops or fake dives or anything?"

Jim laughed. "No, no fancy tricks or stunts. It'll be the smoothest ride you ever had in your life."

"What about lift off and landing? I heard that's always rough."

"No, it's not too bad."

"Maybe for you. What if it makes me sick and I puke all over you?"

"I'll make you pay the cleaning bill," Jim said as he began to flip switches.

The engines roared to life. Gregory heard them and felt them. His heart went to his throat. He didn't want to die. He had told Phillip over and over that morning that he loved him. He didn't want to have any regrets when the plane plummeted to the earth—beyond being in the plane to begin with.

"Phillip is going to be very angry if you kill me."

"Gregory..." Jim cupped his chin and forced Greg to look at him. "Nothing is going to happen to you. I would never, ever let anything happen to you. Okay?"

The fluttering in his chest didn't disappear, but the fear that had been choking him began to subside. "Okay."

"You can trust me."

"I do."

"I want to share this with you."

"Okay."

Jim smiled—the same smile that still had the power to make Gregory feel more than a little giddy—and released him. "Good. Now hold on tight, and I'll get this bad boy airborne."

Gregory took slow and steady breaths, the way Phillip had taught him, and clutched the armrests on his chair. He was calm enough now to appreciate how fucking hot Jim looked in the cockpit, at ease, smiling, the sun reflecting off his hair.

Gregory realized he could distract himself by staring at Jim, and so he didn't look away. Regardless of his own feelings about flying, it was clear that Jim only truly felt at home in a plane.

"You ready?"

"Yes," Gregory lied.

Jim shot him a knowing smile, then began to taxi towards the runway. At first, it was like being in a car. And then it was like being in a very fast car.

And then they were in the air.

Lifting higher and higher. Gregory felt like he left his stomach on the ground. He wasn't sure if he wanted to puke, or cry, or laugh. Jim spoke into his headset and continued flipping switches and studying the monitors. When he noticed Greg was staring at him, he nodded at the window.

"Look how beautiful it is out there. I swear, you'll never view the world the same way again."

It took everything he had, but Gregory dragged his gaze away from Jim and dutifully looked out the window. The view stole his breath, and it had nothing to do with his fear. Everything was so far away, and so small, but so perfect. A perfect world in miniature, and somewhere beneath them, Phillip was working. Maybe even looking up in that moment to watch them fly overhead.

"How you feeling?"

"I'm...feeling pretty good."

"I thought you might like this, once you got over the worst of it."

"I do." Gregory strained forward in his seat, eager to see more. The ride was as smooth as Jim promised, with only the occasional turbulence as they hit pockets of air. "Where are we going?"

"Not far. Just want to show you a bit of the countryside."

"How long have you been flying?"

"Since I was a kid. My dad was a pilot."

"Was? He's retired, right?"

Jim grinned. "Yes. He's retired. He and my mother live a very quiet life in Montana, and he never had a single accident."

"Oh. Okay. Good. That's good for him."

"You're not still nervous, are you?"

"No..." Gregory redirected his attention out the window again. "Not nervous. This is really nice. Being up here with you."

"Does it still feel like falling?"

"No. This doesn't feel like falling at all. I think I love it a little bit."

"Good. You'll grow to love it more."

Gregory didn't have plans to say anything more, but now the words were right at his lips, waiting to be released. He fought them, though, unsure if this was the right time or place. Unsure if there would ever be a right time or place.

"So, who else have you treated to a flight?"

"Oh, nobody. One of the reasons I test planes is that I don't want to deal with passengers. I like to be alone up here. I like the quiet."

"Then why did you offer it to me?"

"Because when I met you, I realized I didn't need to be alone anymore."

"Has anybody ever told you that you can get really sappy?"

"No. Is it a turn off?"

"It might be, if I didn't already love you."

The words hung between them, and suddenly, Gregory
118

wished he had a parachute, so he could jump out the door. Maybe he'd jump anyway, if Jim gave him the *I'm flattered, but...* speech.

"Do you mean that?"

"I do."

"Oh, good. I thought I would have to say it first. I love you too, Greg. Both you and Phillip."

"Really?"

"Yeah. Really."

"I wouldn't have minded if you said it first."

"I planned to, eventually."

Jim smiled, and Gregory felt lighthearted and lightheaded. "I think Phillip is really rather fond of you too."

"Just fond?"

"I can't speak for him. And he's usually a bit...reserved."

"He wasn't reserved last night. I think I'm going to take this plane down."

"Why?"

"Because I want to get you somewhere I can do horrible things to your body without risking a fiery death."

"That's a good plan."

"Well, you know me. Always thinking. I'll tell you when to brace yourself."

Gregory diverted his attention from outside and focused on Jim again. He thought he could spend a lifetime studying the other man, and now he knew he'd have his chance to test that theory.

About the Author

To learn more about Pepper Espinoza, please visit www.pepperverse.net. Send an email to Pepper Espinoza at pepperespinoza@gmail.com.

Look for these titles by *Pepper Espinoza*

Now Available:

Rayne of Love
If All the Sand Were Pearl
Falling in Controlled Circumstances

Print Anthology
A Calling of Souls

Sins of the Past

Amanda Young

Dedication

In dedication to single parents everywhere. I'm in awe of you.

Prologue

Angela sat at the end of the long oak bar, her legs twined in the spokes of her stool. Sipping a club soda, she casually perused the room. She maintained a calm outward appearance, belying the inner anxiety she felt about what she'd dubbed "The Mission".

Nearly midnight on New Years Eve, the club was booming. People drank with excess all around her, half of them stumbling over with it, too intoxicated to walk upright. It seemed the perfect setting for seduction. Following through with her dreams tonight, of all nights, felt especially significant to her. While the others would nurse hangovers and plan easily aborted resolutions in the morning, Angela hoped to celebrate the realization of a dream she'd clutched tight to her breast since she was a little girl.

From across the smoky bar, through a dense crowd of mingling partygoers and the haze of flashing lights, Angela spotted the man she sought. On the outer fringes of the packed dance floor, his tall, lean frame swayed to the earsplitting beat of the classic rock song currently blaring through the club's sound system. His hips gyrated to the music as the petite brunette he partnered tried to keep up with his decadent moves.

His long legs and tight ass were cupped by a pair of snug,

faded blue jeans. Across his broad chest and wide, linebacker shoulders, a white cotton T-shirt stretched to maximum capacity. It highlighted his firm pecs and the slight dip at the center of his corded neck. With every undulation, she could make out the flex and ripple of his washboard stomach beneath the thin, clinging fabric.

Because of the way they danced, the woman hanging onto him like a leech, a casual observer might have assumed the pair were a couple. Angela knew differently.

She'd seen this same man in several of the night clubs she'd frequented over the past weeks. After watching him in action—seeing the way he flitted from one conquest to another without the least sense of attachment—she'd decided he was the perfect person to give her what she wanted.

He always came alone, flirted with every available woman under fifty and left with a different bit of fluff shortly before last call each night. The single thing that made him stand out above all the other men who had caught her attention was his choice of beverage. While everyone else was chugging back one beer after another, he swilled down water like he was suffering from dehydration. She'd never once seen him touch the harder drinks available at the bar. If he wouldn't touch alcohol, it stood to reason he probably wouldn't do drugs either. A handy bit of information to have, Angela mused, when you were searching for an anonymous sperm donor to father your child.

From all appearances, the man was a player. Someone who bounced from one warm body to the next, with little thought of consequence, while spreading his seed to who knew how many women in the process. What difference would one more make when she was ready and willing to accept all the responsibility for the resulting byproduct? It was a win-win situation as far as she was concerned. He would get off—which seemed to be his only objective—and she would walk away with the child she so desperately yearned for.

After setting her sights on him, Angela paid close attention to the type of woman he usually left with. Much like her own too-tall, almost coltish figure, his conquests were all slim and boyish rather than robust and curvy. For tonight, she'd gone out of her way to dress herself in the manner he seemed to find attractive. Newly purchased black jeans, the first pair she'd ever owned, were so constricting she could barely breathe. A low-cut black cotton tank top with a built-in bra pushed her firm, apple-sized breasts to their best advantage. Minimal makeup, a touch of mascara and tinted lip gloss, and her long blonde hair left down to curl in ringlets around her face completed the impression she wanted to give. A representation of exactly the kind of woman she knew he would go for.

In the pocket of her painted-on jeans, Angela fingered the gold coin condom she'd doctored earlier that night. She'd poked numerous holes all along the tip with a sterile needle, hoping they were big enough to allow sperm through, but tiny enough not to be noticed.

Her plans for the future, dreams of having a family, a child of her own to lavish with all the love and adoration she'd never received growing up, rested on the outcome of tonight. Everything had to be perfect. Time was running out.

Ductal carcinoma in situ, fancy doctor's jargon for breast cancer, guaranteed that if she didn't have a child now, before undergoing the required chemotherapy and radiation to fight the disease ravaging her body, she never would. Not naturally.

The chemotherapy would destroy her body, killing any viable eggs she possessed. Sure, she had the option of freezing her eggs. A scientist could remove them, store them, fertilize them in a Petri dish and then, when she was well enough, insert them via in vitro fertilization. The entire time she'd listened to her doctor outline her choices, his voice droning on in a bored monotone as if he were talking about remanufactured car parts instead of her body, she knew that wasn't a choice for her.

More important to her than anything else, even at the cost of her own health, she wanted to have a baby. For a child's love she was willing to risk everything. And if the only way she could accomplish her goal was to trick someone into knocking her up, then so be it. It wasn't as if she could walk into a sperm bank and buy what she needed, not with her medical condition.

When the song playing began to wind down, the end notes lowering in volume, Angela started across the room. As she made her way through the throng of people, she was careful to keep her walk slow and sinuous. The attention her predatory stroll caught, the appreciative glances, were brushed off and ignored. For the first time in her life, Angela was the one on the prowl, a female animal in heat and ready to mate. She was the one calling the shots.

Tonight, with a little cooperation from Mr. Sex-on-legs across the room, she was going to create a life. He just didn't know it yet. And if she had her way, he never would.

Chapter One

Ryan Ward sat behind his large mahogany desk and contemplated the blueprint laid out before him. The landscape proposal he currently slaved away on for Virginia Tech was coming along nicely, but something was missing. Something about the shrubbery he'd intended to suggest planting along the flanks of the building didn't seem quite right.

Rubbing at his temples with the charcoal-stained tips of his forefingers, he closed his eyes and tried to get a clear picture in his mind. He shook his head. No, maybe he would suggest a nice rock garden instead. That would be more appropriate for the new council building they were planning to construct. Opening his eyes, Ryan reached across the surface of his desk for a slim charcoal pencil and a squishy mound of white eraser.

He knew it was rather old-school, but he couldn't stand doing a mock-up on the computer. His creativity came out best on paper, not a monitor. Every time he'd tried to start from scratch on the computer, he came up blank. It was better, simpler for him to do a rough draft by hand and then add it into the computer program later. What was a little extra time when it saved him some grief?

"Why are you here?"

Absorbed in his work, Ryan jumped. His pencil skidded across the paper in a jagged line, ripping a slash down the center. He looked up to see his friend and business partner, Bobby Kincaid, standing in the doorway and staring at him with a pissy expression, as if Ryan had eaten the last jelly donut in the break room.

Ryan frowned. "The last I heard, I still own half of this damn company."

"You're going to be late," Bobby growled, propelling his heavily muscled, six-foot, seven-inch frame into the room.

Ryan glanced down at the cheap plastic watch on his wrist. His sixth one this year and it was only March. Notoriously bad about breaking every one he owned, it made no sense to spend a wad of cash on something nicer. Not when he would probably wash it with his jeans or accidentally drop it into the toilet.

"Late for what? It's only a quarter till noon."

"It's also Friday," Bobby rumbled, propping his hip against the corner of the desk. "As in the Friday you're supposed to be having lunch with the blind date my kid brother Nick set you up on. Am I ringing any bells for you?"

"Shit. Was that today? I'm busy with this proposal. We have a meeting with the college on Monday."

"Yeah, shit. Do you know how much crap I'm going to be forced to listen to if you don't get up off your lazy ass and get across town right now? Nick and that new boyfriend of his, Jake or whatever, won't ever let me hear the end of it."

Ryan laughed, running an errant hand through his shaggy black hair. "So Nick's seeing somebody new, huh? What happened to Rick, or was it Rico?"

"Hell, I don't know. He goes through them faster than I can keep up with. Anyway, it doesn't matter. If you stand up this friend of his, I'm going to be driven slowly insane. And then who would do all the paperwork you refuse to touch?"

"That's dirty, man."

"Yeah." Bobby grinned. "But effective."

Groaning, Ryan stood and shoved back his chair. "I'm moving, aren't I?"

Bobby chuckled. "A little slow, but I guess that's what you old guys call moving."

"Fuck you, Bobby. I'm only thirty-one, exactly two years older than you, my friend. Thirty's staring you right in the face, even if you won't admit it."

"Whatever, man. No matter how old I get, you'll still be older." Cackling like a little old lady at his own joke, Bobby trotted out of the room, leaving the door hanging open behind him.

On his way out, Ryan grabbed his leather bomber off the back of the chair, punched his arms into the sleeves and zipped it up. It was fairly warm outside for late March but riding his hog in the open air had a way of making it feel like winter on the warmest of days. He snatched his chrome-colored helmet off the floor beside the door and slung the chin strap over his wrist.

In a concession to his addiction for donuts, Ryan took the stairs, jogging down three flights to the lobby instead of taking the elevator. He shoved through the double glass doors, stepped out into the brisk spring sunshine and headed straight for his parking space and waiting motorcycle.

It would be tricky, but with just under ten minutes till twelve and a twenty minute ride to the diner where he and his date were supposed to meet, he figured he wouldn't be too late. If traffic wasn't bad and he really pushed the speed limit, there was a chance he could still be on time.

Ryan slid on his helmet and threw his leg over the bike. Kicking up the kickstand, he turned over the ignition, revved it

Amanda Young

up and eased out into the slow midday traffic.

Twelve minutes later, he swerved into the small diner's parking lot, a full set of nerves jolting to life inside his gut. How had he managed to let himself be talked into this? The only people who volunteered to go on blind dates were trolls. He didn't consider himself to be in that category because he'd been cajoled into it. Nobody could lay a better guilt trip than Nick.

He jumped off the bike and strolled across the pavement, taking his time. So what if he was another minute late? Maybe, if he got lucky, the dude he was meeting would be a stickler for dating ethics and would have already left, saving him the trouble of sitting through boring small talk and the obligatory "I'll give you a call" that ended it.

Ryan pulled off his helmet at the door and ran his fingers through his hair, hoping it wasn't standing straight up. He was past due for a haircut, but these days he hadn't been able to dredge up enough reason to care. Glancing in the reflective glass at the door, he was glad to see the wavy mass of black locks only partially misbehaving. Making a mental note to visit a barber, he yanked open the door and sauntered inside.

He glanced around the small old-fashioned diner, with its single row of high-backed, flame red booths and matching red and white checked linoleum. As his gaze roamed, trying to pick out his date, Ryan wondered just whose idea it had been to come here.

It didn't seem like the kind of place Nick would frequent. There weren't any men in black leather loitering around outside or naked pictures on the walls for it to fit in with his demented tastes. This place must have been chosen by his date. If that were the case, maybe this wouldn't be so bad. At least the guy had simple tastes, right in line with his own. As far as Ryan was concerned, there was nothing better than a thick hamburger and a stack of crispy fries.

Being raised in a lower middle class, blue-collar family had shaped him into who he was. Even the success of his own landscape design firm and enough money to buy and sell a thousand of the shoebox trailers he'd been raised in couldn't change his outlook on life. A simple man with simple tastes.

At the back of the diner in the last booth Ryan could just make out the top of a blond head. Since it was the only booth occupied by one person, the rest filled with couples and families, he assumed the blond was his date. Unless he'd been stood up, which was always a possibility.

Feigning casual indifference, he strutted up to the booth. "Hi, I'm Ryan. Are you—?" The blond man turned and gave Ryan his first good look at him. Ryan's tongue twisted, stilling his ability to form coherent words.

The angular planes of his face, sharp cheekbones and a full pink mouth, were cataloged and stored in Ryan's memory. The most brilliant characteristic, the man's luminous blue eyes framed by thick, curling lashes shades darker than his wheat-colored hair, locked with Ryan's and held him captive.

"Um, yes. I'm Andrew." A long-fingered hand was held out in greeting. "It's nice to meet you, Ryan."

Ryan barely had the composure to pull himself out of the limpid pools of blue in which he was ensnared and take the slender hand within his own for a lingering shake. Andrew's hand was warm and soft to the touch, unlike his own rough, calloused paws.

When Ryan realized he was standing there staring and holding the man's hand much longer than was appropriate, he gave it a quick squeeze and let go. He slid into the booth on the opposite side of Andrew and picked up a menu.

Ryan cast a glance at Andrew over the laminated list of the

diner's specialties, trying not to be too conspicuous as he checked the other man out. "So, what's good here?" It was uncanny. The man looked like a life-size version of a Ken doll. Immediately, Ryan, and the cock steadily lengthening against his fly, wanted to find out whether or not Andrew was as flexible as a Barbie.

"Um, well, I don't really know," Andrew replied, with his face buried in the menu. "I've never been here before either."

"So then it was Nick who picked out this place?" Ryan asked, irrationally feeling disappointed that Andrew hadn't chosen it.

"No, I picked it. I hope this place is okay. I wasn't really sure how long this would take…" Andrew finally glanced up at him from around the menu, his cheeks flushed a pale pink that Ryan found adorable. "I mean, I wasn't sure how long lunch would last and I have to be home before my daughter gets off the bus at three o'clock. We live just a few miles up the road in the Rolling Acres subdivision."

Ryan nodded. "Nice area to raise a kid."

"We like it."

Ryan looked back down at the menu, pretending to scrutinize it carefully. He knew the area Andrew mentioned well. It was a high-dollar gated community. Knowing Andrew had money somehow dampened Ryan's attraction to him. He knew it was shallow, but he found himself studying Andrew a little more closely, examining his clothing and manner with a keener eye.

The watch on Andrew's wrist, one Ryan would have normally assumed was gold-toned, now took on a more expensive glint. Since he'd never seen a Rolex in person and had no idea how to recognize one on sight, it could have been authentic for all he knew. It certainly wasn't a twenty dollar department store watch, like the one he sported. The plain blue polo shirt that Andrew wore began to look a little nicer, more designer ilk than the Sears brand Ryan kept in the back of his closet, only to be dragged out and worn for meetings and special occasions that called for something more than his typical jeans and T-shirts.

Ryan tried to recall what kinds of vehicles he'd seen in the parking lot. What did Andrew drive? If they walked out together, would his old, rebuilt Harley embarrass him?

Damn it, he was not going to go there. Not again.

He'd been through this once before with Derrick, the first real homosexual relationship he'd ever been in. Derrick had come from old money. Though he wasn't flashy with it, and Ryan always refused the gifts Derrick bought for him, people had still believed he was using Derrick for his money. The rumors, the shifty glances, all of it eventually drove a wedge between them that neither knew how to fix.

Andrew might be adorable, hot as hell if Ryan wanted to be honest, but there was no chance for a relationship between them. Ryan came from little better than poor white trash. He knew it and he wasn't ashamed of his childhood. His father had worked hard for every cent he'd made. It was simply a matter of the square peg not fitting into a round hole. He wouldn't fit into Andrew's world and Andrew wouldn't want to fit into his.

Ryan decided he would make the appropriate small talk, eat his lunch and leave. The chemistry sizzling between them was better left ignored.

Andrew openly regarded the man sitting across from him while Ryan placed his order with the waitress. When she faced him, Andrew requested the chef salad with Italian dressing on the side before turning his attention back to Ryan.

Although he'd known Jake and his new beau Nick wouldn't set him up with a total loss, Andrew hadn't expected Ryan to be quite so handsome. His blue-black locks, a touch too long and constantly falling into his whiskey-colored eyes, were a pleasant surprise. His tall and stocky build, with wide shoulders that arrowed down to trim hips and long, athletic legs, didn't hurt his aesthetic appeal any either.

Andrew knew from past experience that the good ones were usually reserved for the people who set up the blind dates, not the people going on them. If things went well, as he hoped they would, Andrew would really owe Jake big time for setting him up with this guy.

Maybe he would even be able to talk Jake out of the remaining sense of culpability the man felt regarding their break up two years earlier. It wasn't Jake's fault that the sparks just weren't there. They were much better off as friends than lovers.

Sliding his menu back into the silver-colored holder at the end of the table, Andrew tried to think of some small talk to get the conversation rolling again. For the last few minutes things had grown silent between them, the awkward pause in conversation that only seemed to happen on a first date or a last one.

"So," Andrew started, "how do you know Nick and Jake?"

"Hmm?" Ryan looked up from his hands on the table, where he twined and untwined them, twiddling his thumbs. "Oh. I've known Nick forever. His brother, Bobby, and I were roommates in college before we went into business together."

Interesting. "Business?" Andrew questioned, his fingers toying with his napkin.

"Bobby and I own Ward Creations. It's a landscape design firm."

136

"Oh, I think I've heard of you. Last year, when they renovated the library, didn't you guys do the grounds?"

A small smile tipped the corners of Ryan's thin pink lips. "Yeah, we did that one."

"Katie just loves those little benches in the garden. Sitting out there is about the only reason she tolerates me dragging her to the library as much as I do."

Ryan quirked one black brow. "Katie?"

Andrew nodded. "My daughter."

"Oh." Ryan leaned in on his elbows, his chin resting on the back of his hands. "So. What do you do for a living?"

"Oh. Well...before I moved here, I worked as a commodities broker in New York. Thanks to some good investments, I can afford to stay home and take care of Katie full time."

"That must be nice."

"It certainly comes in handy. Believe me, taking care of a nine-year-old is a full-time job in itself."

The waitress, with her beehive hairdo and pound and a half of makeup, came up to their table, her arms laden with their orders. She plopped Ryan's cheeseburger and fries down in front of Andrew and put Andrew's salad down in front of Ryan before hustling back into the kitchen without a word.

"Got to love the service here," Andrew quipped.

"I'm sure she's doing the best she can," Ryan snapped back at him.

Okay. The muscles between his brows grew taut, trying to figure out what he'd said to bug Ryan. The man couldn't actually think he was really bothered by the waitress's brisk manner, could he?

"Uh, I was just kidding," Andrew muttered. When Ryan glanced at him, Andrew shrugged and added, "About the

137

waitress. It's lunchtime. I'm sure she's just busy."

"Oh, yeah." Ryan reached over and grabbed his plate, switching their meals around the right way, before tearing into his hamburger like it was the enemy.

Andrew glanced down at his salad, covered in a gelatinous mess of ranch dressing when he'd clearly ordered Italian dressing, and on the side at that. Instead of complaining, he busied himself by moving the leafy greens and red cherry tomatoes around with his fork. There wasn't any need to make a big deal out of the fact that he was lactose intolerant and couldn't eat the food he'd been given. He could always eat a sandwich or something when he got home.

"What's the matter? Your food not up to snuff?" Ryan stuffed a fry in his mouth.

"It's fine."

Ryan grunted in reply and Andrew bit his tongue to keep from asking him what his damn problem was. No wonder the man had to be set up on blind dates. He may have been attractive but his manners were shit. Sometime between when he sat down and when their food was delivered, the man morphed from a definite possibility into an asshole. And not the good kind.

Andrew's lips twitched, starting to smile at his own joke, until he looked across the table at his companion. Half his burger was gone and the fries had disappeared completely. Apparently his lunch date was in a hurry.

Fine by him. Andrew snuck his hand into the side pocket of his jacket lying beside him on the booth and covertly dialed his home phone number. The service he used at home forwarded all his calls to his cell. Thanks to the two-way connection he had on his cell, the calls would overlap and as soon as he hung up, his phone would ring. Andrew disconnected the call.

When his cell rang, Andrew shot the obligatory apologetic smile at Ryan and pretended to answer his phone. Hanging up, he looked over at Ryan and shrugged.

"I'm sorry, I'm going to have to cut this short. That was the school calling to ask me to pick up Katie early. It seems she's come down with a little head cold."

Andrew slid to the end of the booth and stood. After shuffling through his pockets, he produced a twenty dollar bill and threw it down on the table. "It was nice to meet you, Ryan." With that, he turned and exited the diner.

Ryan sat, unmoving, and watched Andrew's ass swish back and forth as he hustled out of the diner. The man had a world-class ass. High and tight, just the way Ryan liked them. Small but impressively well rounded beneath the thin cotton of his pressed khaki slacks.

The phone call had been a ruse. Not having been born yesterday, Ryan knew a poorly executed escape plan for a bad blind date when he saw one. Not that he could blame Andrew for taking off.

Ryan didn't know what he'd been thinking when he'd snapped at Andrew for making a lame joke about the service. Okay, so maybe that wasn't entirely true. His mind already made up about Andrew, he'd assumed the man was putting their waitress down. The fact that she really had been rather rude didn't enter the equation at the time. All he'd thought was that Andrew had been looking down his patrician nose at the woman.

Andrew undoubtedly thought he was an ass. And rightly so.

Ryan glanced down at what remained of his lunch, his appetite shot. With a disgusted sigh, he shoved his plate away.

Though their lunch couldn't have been more then twenty bucks altogether, he pulled a twenty out of his wallet and threw it down next to the one Andrew had left. His pride reared its ugly head and demanded as much.

At least the waitress would have a hefty tip to cheer her up.

He and Andrew had nothing in common, no chance of having a relationship. Yet the thought of Andrew believing him to be a boor bothered him.

Shoving away from the table, Ryan rose to his feet and exited not long behind Andrew. He didn't know how to contact the man, didn't even know his last name, but he knew how to find out. Maybe he would send some flowers or something. It was the least he could do for being such a jackass.

Chapter Two

The cordless phone pressed to his ear, Andrew rushed around Katie's princess-themed bedroom. He stalked through the room, trying to make sure he'd packed everything Katie would need for the sleepover she was attending in honor of her best friend Becky's tenth birthday.

He rammed the last of the items on his mental checklist into a gigantic navy carryall. Toothbrush, hairbrush, clothes, socks and panties, an extra set of clothing, pajamas and BoBo the bear. It was all in there.

He hoped he hadn't forgotten something. The last time she'd stayed over with one of her little pals, he'd made the huge mistake of forgetting to send BoBo along with her. A tearful call in the middle of the night had him crawling out of bed and chauffeuring the mangled bear across town to Katie's waiting arms. She refused to sleep without the worn and ragged pink angel bear.

This time he was going out of his way to make sure they did not have a repeat of the last episode. Usually such a well-behaved child, Katie wasn't prone to throwing temper tantrums or crying jags like so many other kids her age. Hearing her cry broke Andrew's heart. Listening from across a phone line and not being there to soothe away her upset was worse. He was lucky there hadn't been any cops around that night or he would've gotten a reckless driving ticket with the way he'd flown that bear over to her.

Now, where had he stashed Katie's pink sleeping bag? He couldn't remember where he'd put the damn thing.

Jake's deep voice blaring through the earpiece reminded Andrew that he was supposed to be paying attention to him. What had they been talking about again? Oh, that's right, the lunch date.

"You owe me big time, Jake. The date you promised would help ease me back into dating turned out to be a disaster. When Ryan wasn't shoving food into his mouth as fast as he could swallow, he was snapping at me or staring down at the table like it was going to jump up and bite him. He's cute, no doubt about that, but a complete asshole."

"I'm sorry, peanut," Jake replied, his voice taking on what Andrew thought of as his mother-hen tone. "I really thought Ryan was an okay guy. I haven't been 'round him much, but Nick talks about him all the time."

"Yeah, well, you thought wrong. That's the last time I let the two of you talk me into going out with one of your friends. The one before this, *God*, he actually thought I'd be willing to crawl under the restaurant table and blow him. What rock do you keep pulling these men out from under?"

"It's not like that, peanut. You know I just want you to find someone and be happy."

"I know. And quit calling me peanut. You know how much I hate that nickname."

Jake guffawed in his ear before Andrew snapped a quick goodbye and disconnected. He really didn't have time to yap on the phone. Katie was supposed to be at Becky's house by seven and it was after six already.

Walking down the stairs, he noticed the house was quiet,

almost eerily so. Never a good sign. He entered the living room and cast a quick eye around the large, empty space.

"Katie?" he called. "Where are you, sweetpea? It's almost time to go."

"I'm in here, Daddy."

In here sounded like it came from the kitchen, so Andrew headed in that direction. When he walked through the partition separating the low-level living room from the eat-in kitchen, he wasn't sure if he wanted to laugh or cry.

Katie had pulled one of the dinette chairs up against the fridge and was helping herself to chocolate cookies. He'd foolishly thought he'd placed the cow-shaped ceramic jar well out of her reach. Clearly not. Crumbs littered the terracotta tile, but most of the damage appeared to be all over her cookie-stuffed cheeks and the front of her pink sweatshirt.

Andrew blew out a deep breath of hot air. "How many times have I told you you're not supposed to eat junk food before dinner?"

Katie shrugged her narrow shoulders, her mouth too full to answer. She raised her pink, fleece-covered arm and swiped it over her chocolate-encrusted lips before hopping down off the chair.

Andrew cringed when he noticed the long brown streaks staining her sleeve. That was never going to come out. Well, at least he'd managed to teach her not to talk with her mouth full. That counted for something, didn't it?

Katie made a big production of swallowing as she trotted over to him. She stopped a few feet away and stood with her thin arms crossed over her chest, batting her long, curling black eyelashes.

"You said I couldn't have cookies before dinner. But I'm not eating dinner here. So it doesn't count."

Okay. And what exactly was he supposed to say in response to that logic? Sometimes he really wished little girls came with a manual. It would make things so much easier.

"It does count and you know it, young lady."

"Nuh-uh," she argued, staring up at him with wide brown eyes. "I might not even get supper at Becky's. The last time I stayed at Becky's, her mom fixed tuna for supper. Tuna is gross."

Andrew felt a smile tugging at his lips at her dramatization and willed it away. It wouldn't do to let her see his amusement. She really was too cute to stay mad at, no matter how hard she tried his patience sometimes. Her long wavy black hair, chipmunk cheeks and expressive eyes never failed to make him smile. He wished he knew where she got her looks. It certainly hadn't come from his side of her genetics.

"How about I let you off with a warning this time if you promise that from now on you'll ask for sweets before helping yourself?"

"Okay." She stuck her bottom lip out in a pout. "Is it time to go yet?"

"Almost. We need to find your sleeping bag first. Do you know where it is?"

Katie nodded, two long braids bouncing over her shoulders. "Yeah. I put it and my pillow on the couch so you wouldn't forget them."

Andrew tried not to smile at the disgruntled look on her face and failed. The way she scrunched up her nose in aggravation reminded him so much of Angie when she was a kid, it was uncanny. She might not look like either one of them, but some of her mannerisms were dead on.

"Come on, kiddo," he said, ruffling her frizzy bangs. "Let's go pick you out another shirt and then we'll get out of here."
144

◆

When Andrew returned home, there was a white van parked in front of his house. Pulling alongside it, Andrew noticed a man standing on his porch.

Andrew got out of his SUV and strode up the walk, curious about who was on his porch at eight o'clock at night and how they'd gotten through security. "Can I help you?" he called out as he approached.

The man turned and Andrew became aware of the floral arrangement he held out in front of him. "Mr. Andrew Vought?"

"Yes."

"These are for you, sir. I just need you to sign for them."

A clipboard, pen attached, and delivery slip was shoved into Andrew's hand. Having forgotten to turn on the outdoor light, he signed without reading and held it out. The delivery guy traded the board for his flowers.

A quick thanks and the delivery guy trotted down the walk back to his van. Andrew watched as he pulled away from the curb before unlocking the door and going inside.

His curiosity piqued, Andrew dropped his keys on the foyer table and flipped on the lamp. Gingerly, he parted the yellow and orange daffodils, hunting for a card. He couldn't remember the last time he'd received flowers.

His fingers stilled around the bud of one delicate flower, a sudden remembrance popping into his mind and lodging there. Of sitting beside an oak casket, the scent of lilies permeating the air as Katie's clammy four-year-old hand tightly clasped his. Angie's funeral, five years past, would have been the last time he'd been sent flowers.

The morose memory cast a pall over his enjoyment of the flowers. Since he would still need to thank whoever sent them, he dug around between the long green leaves until he located a small white envelope. Pulling out the card, he skimmed over the messy script.

Andrew,

Daffodils signify new beginnings.

I'm hoping you will forgive my outburst

and allow us to start over.

Ryan

Andrew slipped the note back into its sleeve and laid it on the table next to the flowers. Maybe Ryan wasn't so bad after all. It was possible that the guy was just having a bad day.

He needed to call Nick and see what his friend would tell him about the man. After he talked to Nick, he could decide whether to call and personally thank Ryan for the flowers or send him a brief thank-you note via USPS.

Ryan lay back in bed, staring at the plastered ceiling overhead instead of the TV currently playing some crappy show he'd never heard of. His mind awash with thoughts better left alone—like being by himself in bed before nine o'clock on a Friday night—he was trying to figure out what he'd been thinking when he filled out the stupid card he'd sent with the flowers for Andrew.

As first, he'd thought to send carnations. They seemed like a plain, *I'm sorry for being an ass* sort of flower. Not too showy or expensive. Then he'd thought roses, but decided they were too senior prom-ish. The daffodils, potted not cut, looked like a perfect in-between flower. Which would have been fine had he not over-thought the card and blurted out a bunch of shit about the meaning behind the flowers and wanting another date with the man.

His brain must have gone on vacation while he'd written the note. That or his dick had hopped out of his pants and suddenly learned how to spell.

That had to be it. He'd let his dick do his thinking for him. Otherwise he would have sent the flowers with a *thank you for lunch* card and let things lie.

What he needed was to go out and get laid. Then the thought of Andrew's guileless, big blue eyes staring up him while Ryan fed the thick length of his cock into Andrew's pretty pink mouth wouldn't be so damn appealing. He was just horny. It didn't have anything to do with Andrew. Anyone would do. *Really.*

This still didn't explain why he was lying on his bed, bored out of his mind, and not out somewhere trying to have his itch scratched.

The phone beside his bed squealed, jarring him from his thoughts. Ryan leaned over and grabbed it off the receiver. "Hello?"

"Ryan? Andrew here, um, Andrew Vought. We had lunch together this afternoon."

Years of practice being smooth fled Ryan's consciousness. His palms grew slick around the receiver and his mind went blank. "Oh, uh, hi." Great, now he sounded like a moron.

"I hope you don't mind, but I got your home number from Nick because I wanted to call and thank you for the flowers. They're lovely."

Think, idiot, think. "I'm glad you like them. It was the least I could do for snapping at you at lunch. I'm not usually so short-tempered."

"I'm glad to hear that. So, anyway, I was wondering if you'd like to try again. Start over with a clean slate. Say tomorrow night, dinner maybe? You can even pick the place this time."

"Sure. I, uh, I'm not sure which restaurant at the moment though. How about I pick you up around seven and it can be a surprise?"

"That would be great. I love surprises." Andrew laughed and the delightful sound lanced over the phone line and straight into Ryan's groin. He swallowed back a groan as his cock thickened, extending to half mast. The hand not around the receiver reached down to adjust his prick inside the loose sweatpants he wore. If Andrew's laugh made him hard, he was going to be in for a hell of torturous ride tomorrow night.

Ryan's hand slipped down to cup his balls, cradling them through the cotton, and squeezed. "Andrew?"

"Yes?"

"Is there anything you don't like? I mean, is there anything you won't eat?" If he said ass, Ryan was going to hang up on him.

"As long as you don't intend to take me to an ice cream parlor, I think I'll be fine."

Ryan could hear the smile in Andrew's voice but had no idea what the man was talking about. "Uh, ice cream?"

"Yes, I'm allergic to dairy."

"Oh. *Oh.* The ranch on your salad, that's why you were picking at it?"

"Yes. Listen, I have another call coming through and have to go. I assume you know where I live, since you had the flowers delivered?"

"Yep." Ryan laughed. "I have your address and phone

number. Matchmaking friends are good for something."

"Okay. So just call me back if you can't find it or something changes, all right?"

"I'm sure I'll be able to find it."

"Great. Then I guess I'll see you tomorrow?"

"At seven," Ryan replied.

"Right."

"See you then." Ryan hit the disconnect button and stared down at the phone in his hand. He wasn't sure whether he wanted to throw it across the room or kiss it.

Lying back against a mound of pillows, Ryan closed his eyes. On his shuttered eyelids, the scenario he wanted to take place the next evening began to play out.

He would take Andrew to dinner. They would sit in a dark, secluded booth and talk. Maybe play footsie and shoot sly glances full of promise at each other over their meal. At the end of the night, Andrew would invite him in and offer him coffee. Ryan would follow him into the kitchen, pin him against the refrigerator and steal a kiss. One long, wet kiss would lead into two and then three. Andrew would break away, his chest heaving under the exertion of his need, and beg Ryan to fuck him right there, standing up against the wall.

He pictured Andrew naked, with his chest pressed to the wall, his back arched and buttocks out. Fictitious Andrew pleaded with Ryan to take him, while reaching back to spread his cheeks wide in supplication.

Ryan's fingers slipped under the drawstring waistband of his sweats and loosely ringed his swollen penis. Up and down, over and again. His fist grew tighter with each stroke, his thumb glancing off the groove just beneath the flared bulb of his cock head.

His free hand palmed his balls, rolling them, squeezing them ever so gently. They began to draw up, hugging the base of his prick, and Ryan changed his touch to a light caress. The soft, slack skin compressed and wrinkled, preparing his load for liftoff.

Faster, harder, his fist flew over the top few inches of his cock where he felt the most sensitivity. Pinpricks gathered at the base of his spine, shot down through the crack of his ass, his perineum and up into his balls, igniting a firestorm of sensation.

His cock pulsed, growing thicker in his hand. His balls clenched and contracted. Fireworks went off. Creamy white jets arched from the tip, spattering his abs and chest with come. Ryan gasped, still shaking from release, and pumped the last of his climax from his softening shaft.

Tomorrow he had a second date with Andrew. A chance to redeem himself.

This time he planned to check his preconceived notions at the door and try to get to know the man. They could actually hit things off, make his fantasy a reality. Stranger things had been known to happen.

Chapter Three

Andrew spent the better part of Saturday cleaning the house and running errands. Doing anything he could think of to keep himself from second-guessing his date later that evening with Ryan.

After talking to Nick the night before and listening to him go on and on about what a great guy Ryan was, he'd decided to bite the bullet and call Ryan to thank him for the flowers. The offer of a second date slipped from his mouth without a thought, almost like he'd been planning to ask him out all along.

With Katie still at her friend's house, he'd called a couple of times during the course of the day just to hear her voice and reassure himself she was okay.

He missed the little twerp when she was gone. Without Katie trampling through the house, her cheerful voice chirping a mile a minute or her favorite TV shows blaring through the living room, the house felt cold and empty. Lifeless.

Although he was nervous, Andrew looked forward to getting out of the house and having an adult conversation about something other than kids and how to raise them. It was disheartening to realize that other than Jake and Nick, he didn't really have any friends. Oh, he talked to people. People at the school fundraisers he volunteered for or other parents, but there was no one he could hang out with and just be himself.

Even Jake had started out as a school acquaintance. Both single fathers and new in town, they'd met at a school PTA meeting. Being the only single fathers there, and later finding out they were both gay as well, gave them enough in common to form a bond of friendship.

Lonely and in need of companionship, they'd tried to take their friendship a step further. Delve into an intimate relationship as well. Not long afterward, they'd found out they simply weren't suited to ever be more than friends. It was a colossal error for them to have striven for more. They parted ways amicably and were able to stay friends, for which he was grateful. In a new town, with no one he knew and a young girl to raise on his own, he needed all the moral support he could get.

In the last few years, Andrew found himself in a dating rut. Actually, it was closer to dating Siberia. Jake, being the great pal he was and much more of a social butterfly, decided to take it upon himself to locate Andrew's Mr. Right.

So far, Ryan was the best of the lot. And with that dismal thought, Andrew glanced at the clock and realized it was almost six. Ryan would be at his house in an hour and he hadn't even showered yet. Unless Ryan had a fetish for the scent of bleach and other various household cleaning supplies, Andrew needed to scrub up before he got there.

Heading for the private bathroom located off the master bedroom downstairs, he ran a hand over his sparse five o'clock shadow. Might as well shave too, while he was at it.

Just because he didn't plan on dropping his trousers didn't mean he wouldn't be interested in a hot kiss at the door. He'd need something to fantasize about when he crawled into bed alone and took matters into his own hands.

Ryan pulled up in front of Andrew's house, a two-story Victorian, and killed the engine. It was a nice home, not too ostentatious, with cream-colored vinyl siding and black shutters. A cement walkway lined with newly budding flowers led up to an ornate front door made of multihued glass.

For obvious reasons, Ryan opted to drive his truck, an older model Ford, instead of his bike. It wasn't new and it wasn't stylish, but it would be a hell of a lot more comfortable for Andrew than clutching his back on the hog. Then again, maybe driving the truck hadn't been such a bright idea. The thought of Andrew's arms around his waist, his groin pressed right up against his ass while the engine rumbled and purred, vibrating underneath them, didn't sound so bad. It sounded downright uplifting.

Snickering at his own corny pun, he pushed open the door and hopped out. He strode up the walk, his head held high, unruly hair brushed and tamed, his best ass-hugging jeans hanging just right.

Tonight would be great. He and Andrew would get along famously and end up in a sweaty tangle of limbs before morning. Everything would be perfect. *It would.* And maybe if he kept telling himself that, the butterflies eating through his stomach lining would go away.

He raised his hand to knock and ended up fingering the glass. Upon closer examination, the door was made from one regular pane of glass, rather than the stained glass he'd thought it was, but it looked like someone had applied several different colored and patterned do-it-yourself stain glass applications. The way the colors melded and the patterns blended together seamlessly was really quite good. It almost reminded him of the abstract art he'd done before giving up on his dreams of being a world-renowned painter and settling on more realistic goals. Like a career that would actually keep him clothed and fed.

He looked up to see the interior door swinging open. Pulling his attention away from the glass, he straightened as Andrew appeared, an amused smile on his face.

"You noticed the door, huh?"

"Yeah." Ryan smiled, taking in the way the snug polo shirt Andrew wore stretched across his shoulders and outlined his well-defined pectorals. Ryan's attention meandered farther down, appraising the creased chinos, and more importantly, the prominent swell of Andrew's package beneath. "It's really good. Did you do it?"

"No. I have no aptitude for art. Actually, the whole thing was Katie's idea. I helped, of course, but she picked out the patterns. It was one of our little weekend projects. She's really creative. I think I may have a future Picasso on my hands." Andrew laughed. "I have no idea where she gets it."

Curiosity got the better of Ryan. He was dying to hear the story behind how a gay man ended up with sole custody of a little girl. And where the kid's mother fit into Andrew's life now. "Her mom isn't into art either?"

"Angie? Oh, no. Angie couldn't draw a straight line without a ruler." Andrew stepped outside and pulled the door shut behind him. "So, where are we going?"

"Oh, I thought maybe we could go to the Dairy King."

Andrew stopped mid-step and looked at him curiously, a crinkle forming between his brows.

Ryan smiled. "I'm just kidding." He ushered Andrew over to the pickup and opening the door for him. "There's a great little

Italian place over on 5th Street. They make a delicious marinara sauce. They even have a live band that comes in on Saturday night for dancing."

Ryan circled around the front of the truck. "Sorry about the truck," he said, as he slid behind the wheel. "It's not so easy on the eyes, but it's a lot more comfortable for two people than the bike I usually ride."

"It's fine," Andrew replied. "So you have a bike?"

"Yeah."

"What kind?"

Interesting. Maybe they had something in common after all. "You into bikes?"

"Some. I...well, I used to be. When I was younger."

"Mine's a 1948 Indian Chief. Rebuilt it from the ground up myself."

"Damn. That's sweet. You'll have to bring it over one weekend so I can take it for a spin."

"Yeah. Sure."

"Damn. I forgot. I don't have my bike license anymore. I never got it renewed after I moved here from New York."

"How come?"

"Well, you know how things get. You get busy with life and whatnot and time just kind of catches up with you. I haven't even thought about bikes in forever. I guess since before Angie died. She always loved to ride pinion whenever I came into town." The last bit was said so low Ryan had to strain to understand him.

"Listen. I'm sorry if I brought up something painful. I didn't mean to be so nosy." Although it was killing him not to ask more about Angie, like what she'd been to him. Had she been a lover, his wife, what?

"No. It's okay. *Really.* Little things just hit me sometimes, you know?"

"Yeah, I understand." But he didn't, not really. Ryan's parents had passed away the year before, only six months separating their deaths. That had been tough, but it wasn't the same as losing a mate. Ryan knew that, even if he hadn't ever experienced love firsthand.

He'd never let himself get close enough to anyone to take a chance on love. Not emotionally. Physically, he'd gotten plenty close to plenty of people, but he'd never opened up. Too many years were wasted, club hopping, bed hopping. Fighting his sexuality by burying himself in one woman after another, just to prove he could get it up for the opposite sex.

Years wasted. And for what? So that he could eventually come out of the closet anyway, admit to himself that he was gay. He was thirty-one and had only been out for five years. All that time, he could have spent looking for his other half, and he'd pissed it away by trying to prove he was something he would never be.

The rest of the ride was quiet. Neither man made more than rudimentary small talk. Safe subjects like the weather or what kind of music they liked, when Andrew began to twist the radio dial searching for a good station.

When he pulled into the restaurant and got out of the truck, Ryan was relieved to have something to do besides think. He escorted Andrew inside and waited with him while the hostess searched out a table and guided them to it.

Their table was in the back, directly off to the side of the small dance floor. In the middle of the white tablecloth sat a vase holding a single, slightly wilted red rose. He hoped it wasn't an omen of things to come.

All things considered, Andrew thought dinner was going well. Other than his depressing comment in the truck, he was happy about the way things were headed.

Their waitress came by to take their orders. Ryan ordered the manicotti and Andrew chose shrimp ravioli. Andrew started to order a bottle of wine, a nice merlot to complement their pasta, but Ryan declined, saying he didn't drink, and ordered a sweetened iced tea instead.

Andrew brushed it off and ordered a glass of wine. It was probably just as well that Ryan didn't drink. One of them needed to be the designated driver.

As the waitress scurried off to fill their order, Andrew turned to Ryan. "So, if you don't mind my asking, why don't you drink?"

Ryan sat back against his chair and was silent for a moment, as if he was trying to decide what to say and what not to. He shrugged. "Alcoholism runs in my family. I guess I always thought it was better to be safe than sorry later, you know?"

"You don't mind if I indulge though, right? I can always change my order if it bothers you."

"No. You're fine."

During their meal, they kept up a steady stream of small talk. Nothing important really, but he did manage to learn some minor things about Ryan. What TV shows he liked and other trivial bits.

Every so often he caught Ryan shooting a lusty glance at his shrimp. He swirled a bit of it around his fork and speared a shrimp and held it out to Ryan, offering him a bite.

Ryan groaned, shaking his head. "I'd love to, but I can't. I'm allergic to shellfish. One taste and I'll swell up like a blowfish."

Amanda Young

"Oh, that's too bad," Andrew replied, a little discouraged his attempt at flirting hadn't worked out like he'd intended.

His gaze milled around the restaurant, looking at other couples relaxing together, enjoying each other's company. That was what he wanted, to be part of an "us", part of a couple.

When his wandering attention returned to his date, he found himself under Ryan's scrutiny. Andrew smiled and nodded toward the room. "People-watching," he said in way of explanation. "It's kind of a bad habit of mine."

"No problem. I catch myself doing the same thing." Ryan's gaze roamed out onto the dance floor. "We could dance?"

"Err, that's all right. I'm not much of a dancer." In truth, he had two left feet, both of which liked to trip him up and send him tumbling straight onto his ass. He could do without that embarrassment.

"Oh, come on. It'll be fun," Ryan wheedled.

"No, I couldn't. Really. I can't dance, never learned how."

Ryan grinned. The dim light caught his whiskey-colored eyes just so, making them appear to deepen enticingly. "It would give you a great chance to check out my ass."

"That's okay." Andrew laughed. "I'll have to take your word for it."

"Are you sure? I have a great ass. You don't know what you're missing."

Andrew couldn't control the snort of laughter that burst free. God, he hadn't laughed this hard in who knows how long. It felt great.

He reached across the table and patted Ryan's hand. An electric shock tingled up his arm, starting a slow burn that wound its way straight to his groin and set up camp there.

His gaze flew up to Ryan's, checking to see if he'd felt it too.

Ryan stared back at him, his eyes glazed and hot, full of the same desire Andrew felt swimming through his veins and filling his shaft to full hardness.

Andrew yanked his hand back. Resisting the impulse to adjust his penis, he placed both of his hands on his lap and held them immobile. "Whoa," he whispered to no one in particular.

Silence reigned for a moment, the static electricity arcing between them until Andrew's self-control hung by a thread. He really, *really* wanted to jump the table and take a bite out of Ryan. See if he tasted half as good as he looked.

Ryan licked his lips, his wet, pink tongue moving sensuously over the expanse of his bottom lip. Andrew's mouth watered. Unconsciously, he leaned in toward Ryan.

"Anything else I can get y'all?"

Andrew jerked back, his gaze shooting to their perky waitress as she approached their table.

"No," Ryan replied, saving Andrew from having to speak over the knot of desire in his throat. "I think we'll just take the check."

She laid their check face down on the table, along with two red and white mints, before hustling off.

Andrew glanced at his watch. It read half past nine. Still early. He wondered if this was it, or if Ryan had something more planned for their evening out. He grabbed one of the mints and busied himself with unwrapping it.

"So," Ryan said. "You want to get out of here?"

And do what? he felt like asking. He didn't dance. Ryan didn't drink. Clubs were pretty much out of the question. What else could two gay men do on a Saturday night?

Hot, sweaty sex?

Andrew shut down that train of thought quick. No sense in going there and getting himself all riled up when it wasn't going to happen. There was a huge stereotype about all gay men screwing anything they could get their hands on. Not him. He wanted a monogamous relationship, wanted to find someone to love and be loved by in return. The empty sex he'd indulged in during his college days simply wasn't enough anymore.

Andrew sighed and gave in to the inevitable. "Sure. It is getting a little late. I guess we should call it a night." He didn't really want the evening to end so soon, but what other option did they have?

Ryan took his time driving back to Andrew's house. He wasn't in a hurry for their date to end and wanted to postpone the inevitable for as long as he could.

Though definite chemistry had flown between the two of them in the restaurant, ever since they'd left, Andrew had been a little cool. Not more than a handful of words passed between them in the last fifteen minutes.

He wondered if he'd done or said something wrong, or if Andrew simply had a case of nerves. He was feeling a few of those jittery, "will he, won't he" vibes himself. Would Andrew invite him in, or thank him for the evening and promptly say good night at the door?

Finally, they reached Andrew's home. Ryan killed the engine and cut off the lights. They sat in complete silence, cocooned inside the truck's cab, their only illumination from a nearby street light that flickered on and off.

Nervous anticipation skittered through Ryan's gut. One of them had to say something, break the tension growing stronger by the second, or he would blow up.

"So I guess—"

"Would you like to—?"

Both men spoke at the same time. Ryan laughed, relieved that he obviously hadn't been the only one trying to come up with something to say.

"Sorry," Andrew said. "Go ahead with what you were saying."

Err. He'd hoped Andrew would go first. What he had been about to say sounded entirely more pleasant than Ryan's intended, "I guess I'd better go" comment.

"I was just going to say that I had fun tonight and hope we can do it again sometime." *There.* That sounded better. And it left Andrew an opening to invite him in, just in case that's what he'd been about to say.

"Me too," Andrew replied.

Awkward silence returned with a vengeance. Damn, he sucked at being subtle. Everything inside him shouted for him to skip the talking and get onto the good stuff. To whisk Andrew up out of his seat and kiss him senseless until there was no way he would be able to turn Ryan away.

Which was precisely why he hadn't gotten laid since quitting the club scene the year before. Being suave was out of his range of experience. In the clubs, he was in his element. Everyone there was on the prowl for sex. If you were subtle, you ended up being overlooked and ignored.

He released his seat belt and twisted around to face Andrew. Ryan gnawed his lower lip, indecisive about how he should respond. Trying to charm his way into Andrew's pants wouldn't work. He wasn't any good at it, didn't know the first thing about how to be charming. All he knew how to do was be himself.

Andrew unlatched his seat belt and laid his hand over the door handle. "Well, I suppose this is good night, then."

Moonlight filtered through the back window, creating a soft, fuzzy illumination which backlit Andrew's strong silhouette.

This was it. If he didn't make his move now, he would lose his chance. Andrew would get out of the truck and go inside.

"Fuck it," Ryan murmured under his breath. Either Andrew liked him or he didn't. He couldn't pretend to be someone he wasn't.

Ryan leaned across the seat and palmed the back of Andrew's neck, burying his fingers in the short, downy hair at his nape. Andrew jerked around, his eyes wide. His lips parted, whether to blast Ryan for his advances or to give him permission Ryan didn't know and he had no intention of waiting around to find out. He swooped in, smashing his lips over Andrew's.

Andrew's back stiffened. His lips softened under Ryan's but remained unresponsive. Unheeding, Ryan tilted Andrew's chin and ran his tongue over the seam between Andrew's lips. He nipped at the sweet flesh of Andrew's bottom lip, trying his best to coax him into returning the kiss.

His frustration mounting, Ryan pulled back. "Damn it, kiss me back," he whispered, their mouths a fraction apart.

Andrew groaned, the sound vibrating up through his chest and pressing out against Ryan's moist lips. Then Andrew was moving, no longer an inanimate bystander but a participant, as his face shifted up and his lips parted under Ryan's.

Ryan took full advantage and slipped his tongue through Andrew's lips, past the barrier of his straight, white teeth, and flicked his tongue against Andrew's. Hot and wet, the inside of Andrew's mouth tasted like sweet ambrosia.

Andrew responded, licking back against him. He caught Ryan's tongue and dragged it deeper into his mouth, sucking on it like it was a cock.

One of Andrew's arms rose, wound around Ryan's neck and tugged him closer. The other settled against his right pec, kneading the tense muscle through thin cotton.

Ryan growled, wanting more. He pushed himself tighter against Andrew until they were hip to hip on the cool leather bench seat and swung his left leg between Andrew's thighs. Ryan pressed the stiff ridge of his cock into Andrew's hipbone, letting the man feel how damn hard and swollen he was.

Ryan was going to implode. Andrew tasted so sweet and felt so damn good in his arms. And his cock throbbed so fucking bad. All Ryan could think of was the need for relief from the relentless ache growing in his balls and the sharp, shooting pulses he felt jumping up and down the length of his shaft.

He dropped his hand into Andrew's lap and ran his fingers over the protuberance of Andrew's cock. Ryan traced the impressive length to the tip and squeezed. Andrew jolted, a tremor shaking his body. The arm around Ryan's neck lowered, his palm coming to rest on Ryan's shoulder. Going by Andrew's response to his touch, Ryan let go of Andrew's prick and reached for the button on Andrew's khakis instead.

Andrew stiffened and shoved against Ryan's chest. "Stop."

Ryan swallowed back the curse wanting to slip from his lips and sat up straight, looking intently at Andrew. The other man's jaw was set in a grim line. Dark splashes of color across his cheekbones betrayed his heightened desire. Eyes narrowed into vivid blue slashes beneath winged brows and a bleak expression marred his chiseled features.

His chest rising and falling under the exertion of each labored breath he drew in, Andrew whispered, "I can't do this."

"What?" Ryan asked in disbelief. "Why? You can't tell me you aren't just as into this as I am. You're as hard as a fucking spike."

"I know. I'm sorry. I just..." Andrew sighed and slumped back in his seat. "Listen, I'm not saying I wasn't right there with you, but I'm just not into casual sex anymore. It's dangerous and stupid, and I have a little girl to think about and..." His voice trailed off as he shrugged.

Ryan sucked in a deep breath, willing his hard-on to go away or at least quit straining against his fly. The zipper was biting into him and it didn't feel very damn good. Probably what he got for going commando. His mind was busy with other things, like trying to wrap itself around what Andrew had just told him.

Not into casual sex. What was he, a girl?

Shit. That wasn't fair. There was nothing wrong with being choosy about who you slept with. Hadn't he quit going out and picking up men for the very same reasons?

"It's not like I don't want to," Andrew continued. "I do. Damn, do I ever. But I need something more now, you know? I want to actually get to know someone before taking them to bed."

Ryan didn't know what the hell to say. His tongue felt like it was broken right along with his dick, which was currently cramped up and contorted in the tight confines of its denim prison.

Andrew laid his hand over the door handle, this time pushing it down into the ready position. Ryan followed the movement with his eyes, assuming Andrew wanted to be prepared to make a quick getaway at any moment.

Ryan didn't want him to get out of the truck thinking he was an asshole who only wanted sex. He wanted to fuck Andrew, he wouldn't deny that, but he wanted to get to know him too. Andrew was only asking to rearrange the order of things a bit. Do the get-to-know-you thing first, and then they could screw. It would only be a big deal if Ryan made it into one.

Andrew pushed open the door, turning on the overhead light. Ryan blinked, temporarily blinded.

"Andrew, wait."

"Yeah?" he said, without turning to face Ryan.

"I know what you're saying, man, and I can respect your wishes. You just caught me a little off guard, is all. I really would like to, um, get to know you too."

Andrew looked back at Ryan over his shoulder. "Really?"

Ryan sighed at the thought of all the cold showers he would be taking in the near future. "Yeah, really."

Chapter Four

Ryan's eyes adjusted to the change in light as he and Andrew left the dark theatre. Jake and Nick tagged along behind them, their arms around each other, oblivious to the curious stares they were getting from people standing in line at the concession stand.

It was no wonder they were being stared at with the way they carried on, pinching each other on the ass and cackling about it like teenagers. Not to mention the way they were dressed. Nick wore skintight, black leather pants and a matching vest. Jake had on similar pants, only in a weird shade of brown, paired with a flowing white poet's shirt. They made an odd couple, with Nick's impressive height, musculature and buzz cut, and Jake's dainty, almost impish features, topped by a mop of wild chestnut curls.

Ryan glanced over at Andrew, who shot him an imploring look, his gaze darting back at their friends as if saying "do something". After the last few dates they'd been on, he'd quickly come to realize that Andrew didn't like public displays of affection any more than he did.

"Hey, Hansel and Gretel, how about you save the kissy-face shit for later?" he yelled back at them, before smiling over at Andrew and shrugging.

"Hansel and Gretel?" Nick laughed. "Where'd you come up

with those names? Couldn't you come up with anything better?"

Ryan shoved open the glass door and stepped out into the chilly night, holding it open for Andrew before answering Nick. "Nope. I think those names fit you both to a T."

"Oh yeah?" Nick spun Jake off his feet and slapped a noisy kiss against his partner's lips. "I guess that makes you Gretel, little buddy."

"Fuck you," Jake replied good-naturedly. "You'd only be Hansel because you're as big as a fucking ox."

Ryan saw Andrew shake his head before starting toward his SUV, leaving Ryan to trail along after him. Since there wasn't enough room in his truck, and Jake and Nick both drove small cars, Ryan had picked Andrew up at his house and from there they'd driven his vehicle. There was more room in Andrew's Explorer so no one had to worry about having their knees crushed in the backseat.

After Andrew released the door locks, Ryan slid into the passenger seat. He watched as Andrew climbed behind the wheel and the odd duo hopped into the back.

Andrew started the engine and cranked up the heat, rubbing his hands together in front of the vent. "So, where to now, guys? It's only nine and I have the sitter until at least midnight. She said she would be happy to stay later if I wanted."

"We could go to The Silver Spur," Nick chimed in from the back.

Ryan glanced at Andrew, curious to see his reaction to Nick's suggestion. Andrew just cocked an eyebrow and asked, "What's The Silver Spur?"

Ryan snorted. "It's a gay bar."

Andrew turned around in his seat to face the men in the

back. "I don't think so, guys. Ryan doesn't drink and I'm not much on dancing. How about somewhere else? We could go somewhere and get a bite to eat."

"Come on, Andrew, it'll be fun," Jake said. "Besides, I remember when you used to dance for me. Your moves are nothing to be ashamed of."

Ryan noticed the nervous glance Andrew shot his way. Now wasn't that interesting. He turned around to ask Jake what he meant and saw Nick punch Jake in the shoulder. Jake punched him back and then they were in each other's arms, kissing, too wrapped up in each other for him to drill Jake about what he'd meant.

Ryan faced Andrew. "I thought you said you didn't like to dance?"

Jake pulled away from Nick. "He doesn't. Not in public anyway."

"Jake," Andrew groaned, "shut up."

"No. This is interesting," Ryan argued. "Keep talking, Jake."

"Yeah, Jake, keep talking," Nick concurred, with a leer at Andrew.

Andrew swallowed. "It's not a big deal. Not even worth talking about."

"Peanut likes to strip. Don't ya, peanut?" Jake laughed.

Andrew twisted around and glared at Jake. "If you don't shut up, I'm going to kill you, jackass."

"Peanut?" Ryan asked Jake. Andrew liked to strip? His cock woke up and thumped against his fly. Now that had some exciting possibilities. Damn alluring, judging by how quickly he went from flaccid to able-to-pound-nails-into-cement hard.

Not so hot was the realization that Andrew and Jake had been an item at one time. He was concerned about how long it'd been since that changed, and how serious things had been between them. Had it been a fling, or something long term? The very idea of Andrew with anyone else irritated him.

Andrew answered before Jake could. "It's a dumb-ass nickname Jake came up with. If you start using it, I swear I'll hurt you."

"He loves to watch all those cartoon specials during the holidays, you know? Made me sit and watch all of them with him and the kids. I thought peanut sounded like a better nickname than Rudolph." Jake cackled.

So things were apparently serious enough for Andrew to introduce him to Katie. The inordinate amount of jealousy he felt over that bit of info aggravated the hell out of Ryan.

He and Andrew had been on a handful of dates, necked like horny teens at the end of every one, but Ryan had yet to be invited inside Andrew's home. How long would they have to be together before he got to meet the kid? For that matter, how long would it be before Andrew let him do more than heavy petting?

He shifted around to ask Andrew about the stripping comment, stopping when he noticed the deep red hue of Andrew's cheeks. Was he actually blushing? He was. And how cute was that? Sympathizing with him, Ryan decided to cut him some slack and not press him for an explanation. He could always drag it out of Jake later if Andrew wouldn't fess up.

"No offense," he said, changing the subject, "but I don't want to spend the rest of my Friday night sitting in a parking lot. So, where are we going?"

Andrew chugged back his fourth—or was it fifth?—shot and grimaced as the tequila burned its way down his gullet. The sting was minor compared to his first drink, so he knew he should probably stop while he was ahead. Much more and he'd be toasted. When you stopped noticing the nasty taste, it was a safe bet you'd had too much.

He slammed the shot glass onto the surface of the scuffed table and sat back against the booth, gazing out over the crowd around him. Music pulsed loud and alive through the dimly lit club. Every few moments a revolving light lit up above the huge dance floor and puked light over everything beneath it, before winking out and casting the room back into dancing shadows. Couples frolicked with abandon, men together, women together, grinding and bumping up against each other to the thump of bass.

Jake and Nick had disappeared almost as soon as they'd stepped through the door an hour earlier. Ryan stuck by his side, though most of the people they saw, from the bouncer to the bartender plus what he guessed were regular patrons, had called out to Ryan by name and asked where he'd been hiding himself for the last six months. Apparently Ryan was a regular himself. Or he had been, up until half a year ago.

During one of the several dates they'd been on in the past month, Ryan had mentioned that he used to frequent bars and clubs. He'd mistakenly thought Ryan meant when he was younger, like in his twenties, not as recently as the previous fall.

Now Andrew sat alone at the single empty booth they'd found upon their arrival, and stared out into the crowd, wondering where Ryan had disappeared to. Thirty minutes before, he'd claimed he needed to use the john, but it didn't take half an hour to relieve yourself.

Andrew was beginning to think he'd been abandoned. In fact, he was starting to get pissed off about it. Shuffling his butt over to the edge of the booth, he was in the process of getting up when Jake slid into the opposite side of the booth and picked up the beer he'd ordered and then left sitting upon arrival.

Jake lifted the longneck bottle and took a long pull off it before wincing and banging it back down on the table. Andrew raised an eyebrow at him.

"Warm," Jake replied.

Andrew glanced back out into the crowd, searching for Ryan's face among the throng of partygoers.

"He's dancing with Nick."

Andrew turned back to Jake. "What?"

"Nick spotted him coming out of the restroom and snagged him out onto the dance floor."

"Oh," he said, too low for Jake to actually hear him over the music, as he leaned back against his seat.

Jake bent forward over the table between them. "You know, if I didn't know better, I would think Nick has the hots for your boy out there." He nodded toward the dance floor. "No real reason I say that, mind you. Just a hunch, really, what with the way he sings Ryan's praises and all."

Andrew flagged down a waitress and ordered another shot. He already had a nice buzz going, but what the hell. He never got drunk. Tonight was as good a time as any to start.

"Have you slept with him yet?"

Andrew closed his eyes and took a deep breath. For someone who was supposed to be his best friend, Jake could sometimes be a gigantic pain in his ass. "We've been dating for a month; what do you think?"

"I think you haven't, which is dumb as shit. The man's a fox. I'd fuck him."

"Who wouldn't you fuck?"

Jake pointed to an overweight man halfway across the room with a bad toupee. "Him," he said, laughing.

Andrew chuckled. Leave it to Jake to make him laugh when all he really wanted to do was glower.

"Why don't you go out there and cut in? Steal your man away from Nick and have a good time for a change. Who gives two shits about what all these drunken idiots think of your moves? Just get out there and make an ass of yourself."

"Gee thanks." Andrew tipped up the last of his drink. "Way to make me feel better, asshole."

"You know what I mean. Go do your thing, peanut."

He returned the newly emptied glass to the table and scooted out of the booth. Rising unsteadily to his feet, he looked down at Jake and smiled crookedly. "I think I will."

"Good for you. Go get him, peanut."

"Shut up," Andrew replied over his shoulder, already shoving his way through the crowd. He had no idea where Ryan was, but he would find him.

God, he was tired. So sick and tired of playing it safe, of being a responsible adult in a world that idolized youth and all the immaturity that came with it. It seemed he'd been an adult since before birth. Even straight from the womb he and Angie had shared for nine months, he'd been the one to come out first, the oldest by five minutes, and the child his parents expected to be mature.

Andrew weaved around bodies left and right. He spotted Ryan and Nick slightly ahead of him and off to the right. Ryan had his head thrown back, laughing uproariously at something Nick was busy whispering in his ear. Breathing a sigh of relief at having finally found them, he shuffled forward. Then he noticed the way Nick shifted closer to Ryan, his hands falling to cradle Ryan's hips as they moved to the music, and molten anger shimmered through his veins.

How dare he? How dare Nick rub all up against Ryan, like some bitch in heat? And why was Ryan just standing there, letting him do it? *The bastard.*

Andrew took a wobbly step forward, his hands balling up into fists at his sides. A man the size of a small mountain stepped into his path, blocking his view of Ryan. He stopped, ready to tell the guy to move the hell out of his way, and looked up, and then up some more. *Damn*, the guy was tall.

At six feet, Andrew wasn't used to having anyone tower over him. Sure, some guys were taller than him. Ryan was an inch or two taller. But this guy, *God*, he had to be close to seven feet or more. He tried to step around the man, only to be stopped by the Amazon's hand landing on his shoulder.

"How about a dance, pretty?" The man's voice was gruff and scratchy, like maybe he'd smoked one too many cigarettes. His words didn't sound like a question, more like an order. Normally that would've ticked Andrew off. He didn't like being bossed around. Tonight, however, it sent a little tingle of excitement shivering down his spine.

Andrew leaned to the side—almost tipped over, before he could catch his balance—and glanced around the goliath. Ryan was still absorbed in Nick's sparkling wit, or whatever the hell it was he found so entertaining.

He turned to the goliath. "Sure." What the hell. It wasn't as if his date would mind. The bastard was too busy letting Nick hang all over him to pay any attention to what he was doing.

"Bud," the man said, holding out his hand.

Andrew accepted the shake and watched his hand disappear inside the larger man's paw. "Andrew."

He started to pull back his hand, but found it trapped in the vise-like grip of Bud's closed fist. Bud smiled, the upward tilt of his thin lips taking away some of the severity from the chiseled planes of his face, and gave Andrew's hand a sharp tug. Pulled off balance, Andrew stumbled forward, his face smacking into the middle of the behemoth's sternum.

Bud's gigantic forearms closed around his back and pulled him up tight against him. Andrew held himself stiffly, not aiding but not exactly resisting either, as Bud began to sway to the beat of the music. Against his cheek, he could feel the steady thumpedy-thump of the man's heart beating. Every granite muscle in Bud's torso flexed and rippled as he shimmied them back and forth.

The song seemed to last forever before it finally began to slow to its end. Andrew let out a breath of relief, glad the dance was over. The arms around him loosened and he sucked in a deep breath, inhaling the pungent scent of sweat and cheap cologne.

It wasn't a bad smell, just not the one he wanted. Not like Ryan. Ryan always smelled of woodsy cologne with a hint of the underlying musky testosterone that exuded from his pores.

He mumbled a hushed thanks to Bud for the dance and spun around, intent on finding Ryan. He didn't have to look far. Ryan stood a couple of feet behind him, his hip propped against the wall, a glower on his handsome face and fire in his eyes. With his arms across his broad chest and his jaw clenched tight enough to grind nails, Ryan did not look happy. He looked mad as a wet cat, and that put a spring in Andrew's step as he strutted over to him.

"Who was that?" Ryan barked out as soon as Andrew got close enough to hear him over the music.

For spite, he glanced back at Bud and waved. "Oh, that's just Bud," he answered as nonchalantly as he could. A smile tugged at the corners of his lips, trying to pop out, but he restrained it.

Ryan humphed and came up off the wall. He moved in close, so close Andrew could count the individual black eyelashes framing his eyes. "If you can dance with Bud," he said, spitting out the other man's name as if it left a vile taste in his mouth, "then you can dance with me."

Andrew shrugged. "I guess so."

Ryan must not have liked the response because his eyes flashed a deeper shade of brown and the grinding of his teeth started up again. The smile Andrew had been fighting broke free and spread across his face. He couldn't help it, seeing Ryan jealous was so sweet. It more than made up for the brief bout of insecurity he'd felt upon viewing Ryan and Nick dancing together.

"You little shit," Ryan muttered, hauling Andrew into his arms and up against the lean contours of his body. "You're getting a kick out of this, aren't you?"

Andrew rested his arms on Ryan's shoulders and sank his fingers into the soft hair at the base of Ryan's neck, kneading the taut muscles. With a contented sigh, he shifted himself a bit deeper into Ryan's embrace, resting his cheek against Ryan's stubbled one. "So what if I am? It's what you deserve."

Ryan's arms tightened around the small of Andrew's back and he began to move, swaying his hips, taking Andrew's body along for the ride. Their groins brushed together with every pass, allowing Andrew to feel how hard Ryan was for him. He swallowed back a groan, feeling his own cock stir at the contact.

Fingertips grazed the rise of his bottom. Andrew shivered, clenching his ass cheeks to stop the needy ache he felt inside.

Ryan must have felt the tremor pass through his body, must have felt their pricks rubbing together as Andrew did, because the riled expression in his eyes wavered and was replaced by something that looked a hell of a lot like more like hunger than aggravation.

Ryan's breath was warm and moist as it wafted over his ear. "I don't think I've done anything to deserve seeing you all cuddled up with that dumb-ass lumberjack. Not when you hadn't even agreed to dance with me yet."

Andrew rotated his hips, pressing in a little harder against Ryan, dragging their pricks together and teasing them both in the process. "I'm dancing with you, aren't I?"

A growl rumbled through Ryan's chest. Andrew felt the vibrations more than heard it, and damned if it wasn't the hottest thing he'd ever experienced.

"You know what I mean," Ryan grumbled.

"Yes, I know what you mean. Just like I know while you were *supposed* to be in the bathroom, you were actually dancing with Nick."

"I went to the bathroom, Andrew. Nick caught me as I was coming out. That's all."

Andrew felt an irrational surge of the same anger he'd experienced earlier at seeing Nick latched onto his man. "He was hanging all over you."

Wait. Had he just thought of Ryan as *his* man?

"He was only talking to me, baby." Ryan paused, his lips feathering over Andrew's cheek. "I do think it's cute that you're so jealous though."

"You're one to talk," Andrew replied.

Ryan sighed, blowing hot air over Andrew's ear. "I don't know what you're talking about."

Andrew shivered, goose bumps of arousal popping up all over his skin. He let go of Ryan's neck, ran his hand between their bodies and gave Ryan's nipple a sharp twist.

Ryan jerked his head back. "Hey! That hurt."

Andrew smiled and snuggled back into place. "It wasn't supposed to feel good."

"Then why the hell did you do it?"

"You were asking for it."

"I didn't ask you to twist my damn nipple off."

"I was hoping it would refresh your memory. Do you still not know what I meant?"

"About what?"

Andrew pinched Ryan's nipple between his thumb and forefinger and cocked an eyebrow.

"All right, all right, I might have been a tiny bit jealous when I saw you dancing with the marshmallow man over there."

Andrew grinned. "Marshmallow man?" That's not how he would've described Bud.

"Yeah, marshmallow man." The petulant look on his face warned Andrew not to contradict Ryan's description, though Bud's body was anything but soft.

He snorted and leaned in to rub his cheek on Ryan's shoulder. Who would have thought he would actually like a touch of possessiveness in a lover? He never had before, but then again, none of the few men he'd been with were Ryan. The man could make anything, even jealousy, look good.

"What? You have a thing for big, brainless meatheads now? You know his balls are probably the size of small acorns because of all the steroids he's taken, right?"

"No, I have a thing for tall, cute landscape architects, who ride motorcycles and get jealous at the drop of a hat."

"Oh really?"

"Mmm–hmm." He leaned up and pressed his lips against

Ryan's, oblivious to the party going on around them. For once in his life, he didn't care if he was putting on a show. All he knew was Ryan and the chemistry and warmth sparking between them like static electricity, the delicious press of their chests and the desire he saw mirrored back to him through Ryan's eyes. "Know where I can find someone like that?"

"Oh I might be able to think of someone," Ryan murmured against the corner of Andrew's mouth.

Ryan's lips covered his, not with pressure but with a gentle coaxing sensation that melted Andrew's knees and forced him to incline against Ryan's chest for support as their lips, teeth and tongues dueled, heedless of the spectators around them. The roof could have caught fire and he wouldn't have cared. All he wanted was more. More of Ryan, more of that one single moment when everything began to slide into place and he realized what he felt for Ryan was growing in leaps and bounds. Steadily spinning away from like and well on its way to another four letter word that should have scared the shit out of him, but surprisingly didn't.

Love.

Chapter Five

Behind the wheel, Ryan listened as Andrew called and talked to Katie's sitter. Hearing a brief chorus of yeses, noes, and thank yous from Andrew's side of the conversation, he had no idea whether or not the girl agreed to stay overnight with Katie.

Andrew clicked his cell closed and sighed loudly. He grinned. "She said yes."

"Thank God," Ryan said in relief. If she'd said no, his dick was going to cry. Just the fact that Andrew had agreed to come home with him and hadn't yet changed his mind at some point during the ride had him hard as iron and ready to burst through the seam of his pants. He couldn't remember a time in his life when he'd ever been so damn horny.

Andrew practically vibrated beside him, bouncing around in his seat, seemingly unable to sit in one place for more than a second before he was twisting and turning in another. Apparently Andrew was feeling the urge as bad as he was.

Did Andrew prefer to top or bottom? They'd never gotten around to discussing it. Sex hadn't seemed like a good subject to broach when he hadn't thought he'd be able to get any. Kind of the same philosophy as the signs the zoo posted, the ones that warned people not to tease the animals. He hadn't wanted to get his hopes up for nothing.

Amanda Young

Now though, after having dropped off Nick and Jake, they were swiftly on their way back to his condo, where a cushy bed and the prospect of mind-numbing sex awaited them. It would be good, of that he had little doubt. As hot as Andrew got him from only being in the same room, it would be damn great. Fantastic. Perfect.

Ryan preferred to top. Had, in fact, refused to let anyone fuck him in the past. Though for Andrew, he thought he might be willing to make an exception. As hot as he was, he would take Andrew however he could get him.

Andrew's hand landed on his thigh, not more than six inches from the source of his discomfort. The heat from Andrew's palm soaked through the denim of Ryan's pants, making his skin tingle and his balls ache like a festering tooth. He spared a glance at Andrew, saw him undo his safety belt and lean across the console, a wicked grin on his face.

"Can I help you with something? I'm trying to drive here." Ryan hated the slight squeak he heard in his voice as Andrew's hand moved up farther. His fingers spanned out over his upper thigh, a scant millimeter away from his balls.

Andrew leaned in, his mouth so close to Ryan's ear that he felt Andrew's lips move before words spilled from his mouth. "Don't need any help. I think I can figure out what to do on my own."

He nipped at the lobe of Ryan's ear. A prompt flick of Andrew's tongue soothed away the sting, but started up a chain reaction in Ryan's body that caused him a lot more hurt than a little love bite ever could. He'd gone past the point of blue balls. If he didn't come soon, his balls were going to turn purple and fall off. He just knew it.

"Andrew!"

"Hmm?" Andrew whispered, his mouth creeping down the

180

side of Ryan's neck, planting hot, firm kisses over every available inch of skin he could possibly reach. His fingers, his bad, *bad* fingers traveled higher, walked right over Ryan's aching balls and cupped them.

"*Andrew!*"

"What?" Andrew pressed a lingering kiss at the corner of Ryan's mouth. "I'm not bothering you, am I?"

"Stop."

Andrew kneaded his balls. Not hard, but with enough pressure to wring a groan out of Ryan. "Why?"

"I'm going to run us into the ditch, that's why."

"No you won't," Andrew said, his hand on the move yet again, deftly working open the button and pulling at the tab of Ryan's zipper. "Just keep your eyes on the road."

With Ryan's pants gaping open, nothing stood in the way of Andrew's fingers as they slipped inside and zeroed in on his cock, folding around the shaft and carefully maneuvering it out into the open air. Freed from the constraint of denim, his prick surged up another inch, throbbing in ecstasy at the extra room to expand and at the tight, firm grip of an unfamiliar hand ringing him.

"Shit. Stop, Andrew, I mean it. There's no way I can drive while you're doing that."

"Sure you can. You just have to concentrate really hard."

Andrew squeezed the base of Ryan's prick and he moaned, the hoarse cry echoing through the vehicle. Andrew shifted and Ryan felt a second hand come into play, wrapping around his cock head and palpitating. The first let go of his shaft and palmed his balls, kneading a bit before moving on. A finger slipped down to rub over his perineum, the very tip whispering over the entrance to his body.

Ryan stiffened, his hole fluttering in response to Andrew's gentle touch. He pushed down on the gas pedal and sped the vehicle up. Only a few more miles and they would be home.

The fingertip pressed in on him, applying pressure, but wasn't quite long enough to enter his ass. It was simply there, teasing him, trying to kill him.

Oh God. Oh shit. He wasn't going to make it. He was going to come all over himself before he even got to touch Andrew.

He gritted his teeth and bit his lip, gripping the steering wheel so hard he was surprised it didn't pop in half. Road signs passed in a blur as he drove more from memory than sight. One more turn, thirty seconds, and he would be pulling into the parking lot.

Up ahead, his building came into view. He swung into the parking lot without touching the brakes, the tires squealing in protest at the sharp right turn. A blunt thumbnail lightly scraped across the tip of his dick, like a match to dry tinder, and Ryan was finally, *finally* able to hit the brakes and come to an abrupt stop.

Before he finished throwing the gearshift into park, Andrew was kissing him, eating at his mouth like he was his last meal and he intended to savor every nibble. Ryan struggled blindly with the steering wheel, tilting it up and out of the way, and he scrambled up, never letting go of Andrew's mouth.

Crawling onto his knees, he turned, pushed Andrew back into his seat and came across the console after him. Andrew's eyes widened and his pulse jumped at the base of his neck. He licked his lips and Ryan knew exactly what he wanted.

One knee perched on the console, Ryan reached down and gripped the base of his dick. He leaned forward, angling his hips down, and nudged Andrew's pretty pink lips with his cock. Andrew's eyes met his, his mouth opened, tongue lolled free, and then Ryan's dick was being vacuumed into the hottest, wettest mouth on earth. Andrew's cheeks hollowed out, and he sucked, hard.

Ryan's eyes fell shut, his hips jerked, and he was coming. "Fuck! Andrew, I'm gonna..."

His orgasm started in the base of his neck, zipped through his extremities and pulsed in thick jets of fluid right out the tip of his cock before he could finish his warning.

Andrew took it in stride, swallowing down his essence without complaint and suckling at his still hard cock until every trace of release disappeared.

Large, misty blue eyes stared up at him in wonder from above the turgid length of his stalk. He should have been spent, completely drained and getting sleepy, but his cock stayed hard, insatiable for more of Andrew. The blowjob was nice, fan-fucking-tastic, but it wasn't all he wanted. He needed Andrew under him, writhing and moaning, screaming his name as he found his own completion.

He cupped Andrew's cheek, shivering as he watched his engorged flesh pull free of Andrew's clinging mouth. He tucked himself back into his jeans and leaned down to softly kiss Andrew. "Thank you."

"Anytime," Andrew said with a mischievous grin.

Between kissing and sneaking quick feels of each other through their clothes, they somehow managed to make it up two flights of stairs to Ryan's apartment, though how they actually got there was a heated blur to Andrew.

His back hit the wall outside of Ryan's front door. The cold surface cooled his backside, even as Ryan pressed against him, heating him from the front. And then they were at it again, mauling each other, kissing and touching, humping with abandon as if the thick layers of clothing they wore were obsolete.

Ryan's hot mouth ran down his neck, busily sucking up a mark at the base, while Andrew panted, trying to catch his breath. Attacking Ryan in the vehicle hadn't been his wisest decision, but he didn't regret it. Touching Ryan, tasting him— like he'd fantasized about for weeks now—had given his hunger a sharp razor edge, heightening it to the point of pain.

Ryan tasted as sweet as he'd known he would, even better really, and he wanted more. Needed everything Ryan had to offer with a fierce craving that demanded remuneration.

A cold hand slipped under his shirt, rubbed over the sensitive skin of his lower back and wormed its way into his Dockers. Ryan's hips rocked forward, pressing their dicks together, as he squeezed one of Andrew's ass cheeks.

"I want to fuck you so bad," Ryan whispered into the curve of his neck, his tongue lashing over Andrew's skin. "Let me? Please?"

Sharp teeth sank into the cord of Andrew's neck. He flung his head back, striking the wall, uncaring about the sting to the back of his skull. "Yes. Oh God, yes!"

Ryan's heat disappeared. Andrew raised his heavy eyelids to see what the problem was. In front of him, keys in hand, Ryan stood grinning. "Don't you think we should take the rest of this inside, or do you have a kink for this kind of thing? After the car, I'm starting to think you do."

"Shut up." Andrew grabbed Ryan by the belt loops and yanked him forward for another kiss. With his eyes shut, Andrew heard keys rattling and the door slam back into the wall as Ryan shoved it open.

"Shit," Ryan muttered against his lips before pulling away and tugging on Andrew's hand. "Come on. Get your sweet ass in the apartment before I end up fucking it out here."

He followed Ryan through the door and into a large, open room made up of white ceramic tile, white walls and glass. Two walls were nothing but unlined windows leading out onto a balcony. Glass shelves lined the remaining walls. Glass end tables framed a huge white leather sectional couch in the middle of the room. Directly in front of it sat a huge flat-screen television. The only things in the room that looked slightly personal were the books on the shelves and the painters' easel sitting off in a corner by itself.

He didn't get the chance to look at anything else because Ryan was up in his face, claiming his lips, and what the man's home looked like was the last thing on Andrew's mind. He was more concerned with stripping down the owner and having his way with him. From the way Ryan's hips shifted, restlessly pumping against his thigh, he didn't think Ryan was perturbed by his single-mindedness.

Clothes began to hit the floor. With an almost collaborative mindset, they let go of each other, leaving only their lips loosely connected, and began to tug things off. Andrew kicked off his shoes, fought with his belt before finally wrangling his shorts and pants down over his hips. Naked from the waist down, his body on fire for consummation, he stepped back from Ryan's scrumptious mouth and yanked his shirt over his head.

Equally devoid of clothing, Ryan stood before him, all long limbs and fluid muscle. Moonlight drifted in through the windows, casting a golden hue over his tanned skin. Broad shoulders tapered down into a narrow waist and trim hips. Beneath firm pecs topped by fat copper nipples was the ripped, washboard surface of his stomach. His hipbones jutted out, framing a perfect V that led Andrew's eyes to his thickly veined prick, which projected out from his body, too heavy under its own cumbersome weight to stick straight up.

Ryan opened his arms and Andrew went into them. Their lips connected, tongues coming out to frolic together. Ryan being a few inches taller than Andrew made the fragile skin of his sac push into the base of Andrew's cock, gloving it, as their hard shafts rubbed together, creating an easy friction with each thrust of their hips.

Ryan's arms wound around Andrew's back, his hands cupping and kneading his buttocks as Ryan began to walk backwards down the hall, leading Andrew away from the living room. Andrew blindly followed, trusting Ryan.

He felt himself being turned in another direction and went with it, too busy ravishing Ryan's mouth to open his eyes and look. The back of his knees hit something and his eyes popped open. He scarcely had a chance to see the bed behind him before he was shoved down onto it and Ryan was crawling on top of him, resuming the frantic mating of their lips.

Jerking his hips up, he pushed his cock alongside Ryan's. They rutted against each other, their mouths connected and sharing oxygen as they both panted. Forcing his hand down between their bodies, Andrew grabbed hold of Ryan's prick and squeezed, pumping his fist up and down the turgid rod. Ryan groaned and rolled off of Andrew. He stretched out, leveraging his long body across the bed to reach into a small nightstand on the opposite side.

He didn't pay attention to what Ryan was doing above. His gaze was too riveted on the flex and play of muscle in Ryan's torso to care about anything else. He reached out and trailed his fingers over the depression between Ryan's hard pecs, following the satiny smooth skin down over chiseled abs to the delicate skin between his hipbones. There the skin grew thinner, more fragile, and was as smooth as the finest silk. He traced the thinning line of hair to the base of Ryan's heavily veined cock, which was surrounded by a thick matt of downy curls.

He ran his fingertips through the springy hair and lightly tugged, bringing Ryan's attention back to him and off of whatever he'd been doing above. Only then did he notice the condom and small flip-top bottle of lube Ryan had retrieved.

The reality of the moment hit him with the force of a sledgehammer. He was really going to allow Ryan inside his body and they were going to make love. Andrew's heartbeat stuttered and his breath caught in his chest. This was it.

Ryan scooted back down to where Andrew lay on his side and pressed a tender kiss to his lips. He pulled Andrew against him and cuddled, his lips feathering kisses on the side of Andrew's face. "I probably won't ever forgive myself for giving you an easy out, but are you sure you want to do this?"

Overwhelmed, Andrew could only nod. His throat was inexplicably clogged by the care Ryan showed in asking such a question. He tilted his head up and kissed Ryan, silencing any further questions he might have asked. Ryan eased the kiss deeper, plunging his tongue into Andrew's mouth and gliding it over and around Andrew's own.

Sight unseen, he took the condom out of Ryan's hand and tore it open. By touch, Andrew figured out which way it went and rolled it down Ryan's stalk, mutely urging Ryan to give him what they both needed so bad. Just to get his point across— that he was through waiting—Andrew fisted Ryan's cock, pumping back and forth, dragging his closed fist up and down the lubricated latex.

Ryan was so hard, so hot, in his hand. What would he feel like inside him? Would he be a gentle lover—take his time and prepare him first—or would he be rough and force his way into Andrew's body?

Ryan's pelvis arched up, seemingly of its own volition, and

thrust into Andrew's hand. Before he could establish a rhythm, Ryan's hand covered his own, stopping him.

"Enough. It's my turn now."

Ryan pushed him to his back. His mouth blazed a trail of hot, moist kisses over his collarbone and down his chest. Andrew closed his eyes, arching into Ryan's touch, as his nipples were laved with the flat of Ryan's tongue. Always sensitive, his nipples crinkled and drew up tight as one and then the other was tormented by Ryan's softly abrasive tongue. Andrew writhed on the bed, his mind insensate as his hips rocked back and forth, all the nerves in his body at attention.

Awash in sensation, he barely heard Ryan flip open the cap on the lube and squeeze out a slippery dollop of the fluid. He did feel the cool liquid and Ryan's warm fingers brush through the valley between his buttocks. A wide finger nudged his anus and Andrew stiffened, freezing more out of instinct than thought.

"Easy, baby, just let me loosen you up a bit."

Ryan's husky voice whispering in the dark was better than a muscle relaxant. Andrew took a deep breath and willed his body to open, to let Ryan in. The insistent finger slipped inside, breaching the portal with little resistance. A second finger worked its way in beside the first. Andrew gasped at the slight burn of unused muscles being forced to spread.

It had been so long...

The digits inside him twisted, plunging in and out before they disappeared, leaving him empty and aching to be refilled. "Ryan. Please. I need..."

Ryan moved above him, crouching between his splayed thighs. "It's okay, baby. I'm here. I'm going to give you what you need."

"Please, Ryan. Now."

Ryan's hands on him were gentle as he gripped Andrew's bottom and parted his cheeks. Andrew watched as Ryan took hold of his latex-sheathed prick and lined it up with the entrance to his body. He felt the blunt head probe at his hole, exerting pressure, and inhaled, pushing out. The wide flare of Ryan's cock popped through the defiant ring of muscle. Andrew cried out, whimpering at the delicious burn of Ryan inside him. His hands fisted in the coverlet, holding on while he waited for the final shove that would seat Ryan completely within him.

Letting go of Andrew's ass, Ryan bent down, putting all his weight on his arms at either side of Andrew's head, and kissed him. "Ready?"

"Yes. God, yes. Just do it. Fuck me."

Andrew lifted his legs and wrapped them around Ryan's hips. Ryan buried his face in the curve of Andrew's neck, his respiration fast and choppy, and thrust home.

"Ryan!"

Buried to the balls, Ryan held himself still while Andrew tried to adjust to the huge battering ram shoved inside him.

"Oh God, Drew. So hot, so tight. You feel so damn good, baby."

Andrew booted Ryan's ass, trying to get him to move, to do something to make the ache, the intense pressure, go away. He was so close, needed to come sooo bad. It wouldn't take much to send him over. "Move! Fuck me, damn it."

Ryan chuckled, the vibrations in his diaphragm echoing down and through his cock, straight into Andrew's stretched and burning hole. Andrew whimpered, rocking his hips up, trying to assuage the need clawing at him. He squeezed down, clutching Ryan's hard flesh with his rectal muscles.

Ryan moaned as his pelvis jerked backward and surged forward, dragging his swollen cock through sensitive, nerve-rich

189

tissues. In and out, on and on, he rapidly plunged into Andrew. Every thrust grew rougher, more frantic.

Ryan twisted his hips, changed his entry, and his cock brushed over Andrew's gland. Andrew bucked, crying out as his balls drew up and all the muscles in his groin locked down. Fire licked over his scrotum, his back arched, and he came and came and came some more. The contractions went on unabated, driving him to the brink of sanity. Ryan went rigid above him, his cock growing impossibly bigger, and then he was coming as well.

Ryan rid himself of the condom, tied it off and pitched it into the wastebasket near his bed. He rolled to his side and took Andrew with him, snuggling Andrew's head into the crook of his arm. "Damn. That was..." He searched for a word, but couldn't come up with anything that would describe the mind-blowing experience they'd just shared. He settled for "Wow." Maybe when all the blood in his lower body rejoined his brain he would be able to do better. Until then, "wow" would have to suffice.

Andrew chuckled against his neck. "Yeah, I would say *wow* describes things just fine." His lips pressed a quick kiss against Ryan's rapidly cooling skin.

It was still getting a bit chilly at night and, once again, he'd forgotten to turn on the heat in his apartment. Ryan wiggled around until he found the edge of the quilt on his bed and could tug the end over them. Cocooned in the cover with Andrew wrapped around him like a clinging vine, Ryan settled back and floated in the moment. Life didn't get much better than this.

The tenor of Andrew's voice broke through Ryan's tranquility. "Can I ask you something?"

"Sure."

"Did you decorate this place or did it come furnished? I mean, uh, it's nice and all, but it doesn't really look like you."

Ryan smiled. "Yeah, I said the same thing when I saw it. My kid sister, Lisa, is majoring in interior design in college and begged me to let her do the place when I bought it last year. I made the mistake of agreeing. She chose pretty much everything in the place except for the TV. That was my doing. Why do you ask?"

"Just curious I guess. So you just have the one sister?"

"Yep. It was just me and Lisa. What about you?"

"No. I, um... Well, my twin sister, Angie, passed away a few years ago."

Angie? Wasn't that the name of his little girl's mom too? "I'm sorry. That must have been rough. If you don't mind my asking, how did she pass?"

"A drunk driver sideswiped her car one night when she was on her way home from work."

"That's terrible."

"Mmm-hmm," Andrew replied, burrowing into his side. "Can we talk about something else?"

"Sure. There's something I've been wanting to ask you anyway."

"That sounds ominous."

"Not at all. I've just been wondering where Katie's mom is, and why she isn't helping you out. I don't think I've ever heard you mention her."

Andrew squirmed around until Ryan lifted up and let him have his arm back. He propped himself up on it and stared down at Ryan with eyes shrouded in misery. "Angie, my sister, is Katie's mom. When she died, she left me custody of Katie."

Well, that certainly solved that mystery. "What about her dad?" Andrew winced, causing Ryan to rephrase his question. "I mean her biological father. Where is he?"

"I don't know. Angie never told me who Katie's father was. To be perfectly honest, I'm not sure she even knew. I always got the feeling Katie was the product of a fling, you know? Anyway, it doesn't really matter now. I love Katie as much as any blood parent could. She's my daughter."

Chapter Six

Spring changed to summer and school let out. Katie was home twenty-four/seven, which made spending time with Ryan damn near impossible.

Andrew was at his wit's end, trying to work his and Ryan's relationship around his life. They had now been together for almost four months, and he figured the time had come to move their relationship along. It was time to introduce Ryan to Katie.

Thinking it would be less awkward, Andrew arranged to have a barbeque at his house, inviting only Ryan and a few select friends. Mostly people Ryan and Katie both knew and would feel comfortable around. Though he didn't plan to explain the ins and outs of his and Ryan's relationship to Katie, just introduce him as a friend, somehow having other people around felt less conspicuous.

He was afraid if he simply brought Ryan home with him one evening, it would lead to questions he wasn't ready to answer. Questions about the birds and the bees and why Daddy didn't like birds as well as other bees like him. Katie was far too young for that talk. And he sure as hell wasn't ready to give it. By his estimation, Katie would be ready for the sex talk sometime around the year she hit thirty. Maybe not even then.

It did make him wonder how other single parents could carry on a private life without letting their kids in on it. He knew some people didn't have a problem with running a never-ending stream of partners past their children, but he wasn't one of them. Katie having a stable and loving home, devoid of myriad "uncles" passing through, was more important to him than his own social life. To his way of thinking, what with losing her mom and then being saddled with her clueless gay uncle, Katie had been through enough. As her only parent, it was up to him to see that she was protected and sheltered.

Hence, the reason she had yet to meet Ryan. Now that he'd made his mind up about introducing them, he was terrified they wouldn't get along. He prayed he wasn't moving things too fast and making a mistake by letting Ryan meet her.

Ryan had no experience with kids, he'd admitted as much himself, and while Andrew knew he'd be on his best behavior around Katie, there was still the fear that they would hate each other. If that turned out to be the case, he wasn't sure what he would do. Katie was his world, and Ryan was steadily worming his way right into the same stratosphere.

Which was one of the reasons his palms were sweaty and his knees shook as he scrambled around the kitchen making sure things were ready. He glanced down at his watch. Almost eleven-thirty. People were due to start showing up any time now. He'd told everyone twelve, but he knew better than to expect half of them not to show up early.

The night before, he'd stayed up late baking a cake for the grownups and cupcakes for the kids. Hotdogs and hamburgers were on a tray in the fridge, waiting to be grilled. He'd bought a tub of potato salad from the market. He'd never been any good at making things that didn't have a set recipe. Anything that called for a dab or pinch of something was beyond his meager cooking capabilities.

While he added a bit more multicolored sprinkles on top of

the cupcakes, Katie darted into the kitchen, a tiny whirlwind of motion in a pink shorts set with a unicorn on the front of the tee. She stopped beside him, her fingers reaching out to make a pass through the chocolate icing he'd only then finished spreading over the cake. Andrew caught her hand mid-swipe and wiped it off with a dish towel.

"No sweets until you've eaten something else."

"Aw. You're no fun, Daddy. Becky's mom always lets her lick the bowl."

"Do I look like Becky's mom?"

Katie giggled and made another swipe at the icing. "No, silly, you're a boy."

"Ah-ah-ah." Andrew laughed, catching Katie under the arms and swinging her away from the cupcakes. "Don't you remember what happens to bad little girls who don't listen to their daddies?"

"No," she said, squirming and giggling, though they'd played this game for years. "What happens?"

Andrew growled and blew a raspberry on her cheek. "The tickle monster gets them."

Katie squealed in peals of laughter and wiggled harder. "No. No, Daddy, I'm too old for the tickle monster!"

Andrew ignored the fake protest and started tickling Katie under her arms, where she was the most ticklish. Katie dropped to her side on the floor, rolling up into a wiggly ball of giggles.

"Stop, Daddy. I'm gonna pee."

Grinning like a loon, Andrew quit tickling Katie and pulled her off the floor. Once he had her on her feet, he smacked her on the bottom and pointed toward the living room. "Why don't you go watch some cartoons until Shawn gets here? Then the two of you can go outside and play."

Luckily enough, it was Jake's weekend to have Shawn, his eight-year-old son. He planned to bring him along to give Katie someone closer to her own age to play with.

"Okay," she said over her shoulder, running off to watch whatever cartoons were on. Andrew was glad he'd had the satellite installed. There were a lot more cartoon channels to keep Katie occupied with than there were on regular cable. He didn't know when the local channels had stopped playing cartoons on Saturday morning the way they had when he was a kid. Hearing the theme song for SpongeBob echo through the house, Andrew smiled and turned to put the finishing touches on lunch.

Ryan parked behind Jake's Honda and blew out a nervous breath. He didn't see Nick's beat-up old Mazda, so he must have ridden with Jake or Bobby. Everyone was already inside, doing whatever people did at a barbeque.

Cannibalistic butterflies ate at his guts, chowing down on his insides while he worked up the nerve to get out of his truck. He didn't know why he was so antsy; it was only one little girl he was supposed to meet. Everyone else he already knew and liked. That was the crux of the problem right there. What if he didn't like the kid, or she was a spoiled brat who took an instant dislike to him? Andrew loved his kid and Ryan knew that if it came right down to it, he would be the one given his walking papers. He was falling in love with Andrew, so making a good impression with his kid was paramount.

This was why he'd stopped on his way over and picked up a stuffed animal, though the detour made him arrive later than he would've liked. Kind of the same principle as bringing flowers for someone's mother, really. Instead of flowers, he'd bought the kid a pink stuffed elephant. Hopefully it wasn't too immature a gift for a nine-year-old. He'd looked at Barbie dolls and some of the other crap, but there had been so many different things. And he didn't know beef from bullshit about what a girl would like. The elephant seemed like a safe bet at the time. Now he wasn't so sure.

Brushing off his insecurities, Ryan opened the truck door and hopped out. He walked over to the passenger side and leaned in through the open window to grab the pot of cocktail wieners and barbeque sauce he'd made for the potluck and the stuffed animal. Shoving the elephant under his arm, he started up the walk.

The door was open so he walked on in, his gaze taking everything in. From where he stood in the foyer he saw stairs leading up to the second floor on his right, a sunken living room decorated in shades of blue off to his left, and what looked to be a kitchen with white terracotta tiles straight ahead. Muted noises of people laughing and a dog barking floated on the air.

Ryan headed in the direction from which the noise came, the kitchen. Entering the room, he noticed an open back door. Everyone must have been outside. He set down his dish and approached the door. Looking out, he saw Andrew and Jake by a large brick grill, arguing over the best way to line up the charcoal. Bobby and his girlfriend, Sherry, were sitting at the picnic table, laughing up a storm as they pointed at Nick and two little kids who were rolling around on the grass with a tiny, fuzzy, tan-colored puppy.

He guessed the little girl was Katie, though he wouldn't have been able to pick her out of a line up as being Andrew's child. She looked nothing like him. Andrew had light blond hair and vivid blue eyes. His daughter had deep brown pigtails and big amber eyes. Even their skin tone was different, Andrew's being peaches and cream and Katie's closer to Ryan's own tan complexion. The boy was obviously Jake's son. He was the

197

spitting image of his father with curly chestnut hair and impish gray eyes.

He must have made a sound or something because Andrew turned from his discussion with Jake and spotted him standing in the doorway. A smile spread across his face. He lifted a finger at Ryan, motioning for him to wait where he was for a minute, then turned and said something to Jake while pointing at the kids. Jake glanced over his shoulder at Ryan, a Cheshire cat grin on his face, and nodded. Andrew handed him the bag of charcoal he was holding and began to stride toward Ryan.

"Hey," Andrew said, pushing Ryan deeper inside the room while nudging the back door closed with his hip. "I didn't think you were ever going to get here. Everyone else showed up half an hour early, while the one person I wanted to see most comes strolling in almost an hour late."

Andrew pushed him back against the closed door and kissed him. What started out as a slow and easy "hello" kiss quickly morphed into a raging inferno. Ryan teased Andrew's tongue into his mouth and sucked on it, emulating what he'd rather be doing to his sweet prick. Andrew pulled back, his chest heaving, and placed his hands on Ryan's chest to stop him.

"Not here. The kids are outside."

"You started it. You little tease."

"I know. I'm sorry, I just missed you. Feels like forever since we've had any time alone."

"Yeah." Ryan bent to pick up the elephant he'd dropped to the floor in his quest to swallow Andrew's face. "Listen, I'm sorry I'm late. I thought I should bring something for Katie, but then I got in the store and couldn't make my mind up about what to get." He held out the stuffed animal. "Do you think this is okay, or is it too hokey?"

"I'm sure she'll love it. She's going through a pink phase." He shook his head, smiling. "Absolutely everything has to be pink. If it weren't so nauseating, it would be cute."

"I'll bet," Ryan said, shoving his hands in his pockets. "So, um, I know you said I didn't have to bring anything, but I thought since everyone else was... Anyway, I'm not much of a cook, so I just did cocktail weenies. Hope that's okay?"

"Yeah, that fine. Great, actually; no one else did those. Why don't you carry them out to the picnic table while I grab some more starter fluid? Jake's determined to go through a case of the stuff before he actually manages to start a fire."

"Yeah, well, uh, I'll just go outside then."

"'Kay, I'll be out there in a sec."

Ryan grabbed his wieners and walked outside, leaving the elephant sitting on the counter. He assumed Andrew planned to introduce him to Katie at some point and he didn't want to take the stuffed animal outside and take a chance on getting it dirty before he had the chance to give it to her.

He approached the picnic table and set down his offering. Bobby leaned over and lifted the lid, peeking inside, while Ryan straddled the bench opposite him and Sherry.

"Hey, Ryan," Sherry said with a small smile. "Long time, no see."

"Yeah, it's been awhile, hasn't it?" Ryan's attention diverted to Bobby, who was in the process of plucking a sausage out with his fingers. He swatted Bobby's hands away from the dish. "Get your grubby mitts off that. No one wants to eat something you've stuck your fingers in. It's hard to tell where they've been this morning."

Bobby grinned and sat back down next to Sherry, wrapping one of his beefy arms around her. "Aw, come on, man. I'm starving and I just love those little wieners."

"Sounds like a personal problem to me, bud." Ryan laughed and Bobby turned three shades of red when he realized what he'd said.

From that point on, Ryan loosened up and actually found himself enjoying the barbecue. When the meat was grilled and everybody lined up to fill their plates, Andrew finally pulled him aside.

Andrew must have seen the pulse jump in his neck, because he leaned in as they approached the kids and whispered, "You ready?"

"I guess so." Ryan chuckled. "Who would have thought I'd be so nervous about meeting your kid?"

"She's just a little girl. She doesn't bite. Much."

"Very funny, Mr. Comedian."

"Katie, Shawn, come over here. It's time to eat and you two need to go in and wash up. You have puppy slobber all over you."

"Daddy!" Katie ran up and threw her arms around Andrew, practically knocking Ryan out of her way to get to her dad. "Shawn's puppy is so pretty and cuddly. Can I have a puppy? Can I, please? I'll take extra good care of him and I'll—"

Andrew sighed and rolled his eyes heavenward. Ryan watched the byplay between father and daughter with thinly disguised amusement. He could remember driving his dad crazy asking for a dog too. Though his reasons for not getting a pet had more to do with their family not being able to afford another mouth to feed, even a canine one, as opposed to whatever possible reason Andrew was reluctant to buy her a pet.

"We've already talked about this, Katie. We don't need a dog right now. Maybe we can get one in a couple of years, when you're older."

"Daddy! You've been saying that forever. When will I be old enough?"

"Not for a couple of years yet, sweetpea."

"But, Dad—"

"Not right now, sweetpea. We'll talk about it later. Now, come on over here, there's someone I want you to meet."

Dragging her feet through the grass, Katie trudged over toward them.

"Katie, this is my friend Ryan."

"Hi," she said, holding out her little hand. "My name is Katie Rhiannon Vought. It's nice to meet you."

Impressed, Ryan bent down and gingerly shook her tiny hand. "It's very nice to meet you too, Katie. Your dad talks about you all the time."

"He does?"

Ryan nodded. "Yep."

"What does he say 'bout me?"

"Oh, well, just how lucky he is to have such a special little girl and how pretty you are."

Katie fluttered her lashes up at him and tucked in her narrow shoulders, as if she were embarrassed by the compliment. Ryan snickered at her coquettish act. From what he'd seen so far that afternoon, there wasn't a bashful bone in the kid's body.

"Katie, take Shawn into the house and wash your hands. After you eat, there are cupcakes waiting for you. And, Katie, I believe Ryan left a present for you inside on the counter."

"A present?" she squealed, her eyes lighting up.

She ran over to Shawn where he was petting his dog, and latched onto his wrist. "Come on, Shawn. We gotta go clean up.

Dad says we have dog cooties."

Ryan rose to his feet, watching as the kids ran toward the house. He distinctly heard Shawn telling Katie that puppies didn't have cooties. Only girls had those.

"Great kid," Ryan said, looking at Andrew.

"I know, right?"

The two of them wandered over to the table and fixed plates for themselves. Ryan sat down and ate, keeping an eye on Andrew while he fixed a plate for Katie and made sure she was settled before joining him.

Everybody, including Ryan, made pigs out of themselves on the good food. When he went back for thirds, he didn't feel even a twinge of hoggishness. It had been awhile since he'd had a good home-cooked meal. Most of the time he lived on takeout or microwavable stuff.

His plate clean, his belly ready to bust, Ryan stretched and yawned. He looked around for Andrew and spotted him standing next to a tree, watching Nick and Jake throw horseshoes. Katie and Shawn were a little ways behind them, content to play with the puppy. Ryan felt a zing of pride when he noticed Katie held onto the toy he'd bought her and was showing it off to the dog.

Ryan strolled up to Andrew and leaned against the tree beside him. "I think I need to use the little boy's room myself." Ryan waggled his eyebrows. "Want to show me where it is?"

Andrew laughed. "Yeah, just let me get Jake to keep an eye on the kids while we're inside."

In the blink of an eye they were in the house, in Andrew's bedroom, and Ryan had Andrew shoved up against the wall, devouring his mouth with all the pent-up desire he'd stored up since they'd last seen each other.

He hoped now that he'd met Katie, Andrew would let him come around more often. Surprisingly, it would even be okay if they couldn't do anything sexual. Over the past few months, he'd come to realize just being in Andrew's presence, talking and hanging out, was more gratifying than fucking someone else. He truly enjoyed being around the man.

Andrew sucked on his bottom lip, nipped it with the sharp edge of his teeth, and Ryan groaned, no longer thinking about anything but the warm, hard body rubbing up against him and the intoxicating flavor of Andrew's kiss. He reached around and grabbed two handfuls of prime cut, grade A ass, and squeezed. Andrew must have liked that because his hips rocked forward, pressing his long, hard cock right into the cradle of Ryan's pelvis, and ground against him. His cock was engorged and throbbing, begging for the touch of something other than his own hand. Something only Andrew could provide.

Without a care for the world around them, Ryan dropped to his knees and started working at the buttons on Andrews button-fly khakis. He absently wondered if the man ever wore anything other than slacks. And then he wasn't thinking, because Andrew's pretty pink cock was shooting up through the opening in his fly and Ryan was swallowing him down.

He dug his tongue into the tiny slit in the head and savored the bittersweet drop beading there. Andrew grabbed the back of his head, his fingers twining in his hair, as he thrust his cock deeper into Ryan's mouth. Ryan groaned around the smooth, spongy flesh and sucked him in, taking him all the way to the back of his throat before moving up. Again and again, he shuttled Andrew's prick in and out of his mouth. On the upstroke, he laved the tender depression beneath Andrew's helmet with his tongue. On the downstroke he licked and swirled his tongue over the puffy blue vein running down the underside of his shaft.

Every groan that spilled from Andrew's mouth was a sweet benediction. Ryan could do this forever. Spend the rest of his days on his knees, loving Andrew with his mouth.

Love? Oh, shit! Could what he felt actually be love? Was he in love with Andrew?

The implications of what he was feeling pointed to yes. Ryan's pace slowed, his suction all but stopping. He glanced up at Andrew, who stared back down at him, his face flushed and his beautiful blue eyes heavy. That single look was all it took for him to know. *Fuck.* He was in love with Andrew.

Chapter Seven

Ryan let Andrew's cock slip from between his lips. He studied the moist, gleaming appendage with regret before turning his attention to its owner. An incredulous expression appeared on Andrew's face when he realized Ryan had no intention of taking it back in his mouth, but he didn't say anything.

Never one for beating around the bush, Ryan desperately wanted to tell Andrew what was on his mind. He just had to figure out how to go about doing it. Ryan knew Andrew had feelings for him; he simply wasn't sure what those feelings were. Having only then realized he was in love with Andrew, Ryan yearned to say the words out loud, but was afraid of what Andrew's reaction would be. His timing was shitty, but that couldn't be helped. The emotions bottled up inside him were too strong to ignore.

Ryan opened his mouth, ready to throw his feelings out on the table. "Andrew, I—"

A loud bang hit the side of the house, interrupting him. Andrew cursed and jerked away from him. Ryan stood and watched as Andrew hastily stuffed his dwindling erection back into his pants.

"Shit. I have to go see what that was." He shot a sympathetic moue at Ryan. "We probably shouldn't be messing around in here right now anyway."

Slightly miffed about having his confession cut short, but trying his best to be understanding, Ryan sighed. "I know. Um, about that bathroom though...?"

Andrew pointed to a closed door on the back wall. "You can use mine. It's right behind you." He pressed a fast, chaste kiss on Ryan's lips and hustled out of the room.

"And aren't you just smooth?" Ryan said aloud to the empty bedroom as he walked into the bathroom and relieved himself. "Try to tell someone you're in love with him and he runs out of the room like his ass is on fire. Way to go, me."

Exiting, he looked around Andrew's bedroom. Everything was decorated in shades of beige and navy blue. The king-size sleigh bed and matching nightstand and dressers were made of cherry and gleamed with polish. Atop the bureau sat a bottle of the cologne Andrew favored, a small, clear jar with change in it and several framed photos of different sizes. They were mostly of Katie at varying ages but one in particular, near the back, caught his eye.

Picking up the heavy silver frame, he studied the image of a younger Andrew and a young blonde woman who had to be Angie, since she was practically the female version of Andrew. Angie's arm wrapped around Andrew's waist and his lying across her shoulders, they smiled cheerfully into the camera. Both had the same color hair and eyes, the same tall and athletic build. The only difference he could discern was their nose. Andrew's was a tad on the large side, with a tiny hump in the middle, while Angie's was smaller and tip tilted. She also had an abundance of freckles across the bridge of her nose and her cheeks that Andrew lacked.

Something about her nagged at Ryan's subconscious. Andrew's sister looked really familiar to him. He studied her features closely, thinking maybe it was simply the way she favored Andrew that struck a chord within. A chill crept down Ryan's spine and he realized why she looked so familiar. Angie was Angela. A quick, one-night stand he'd participated in over a decade before. His eyelids drooped as he remembered picking her up in one of the seedy bars he'd frequented.

Her face probably would have blended into the mix with the other women, all but for the night he'd slept with her being New Years Eve and the resolution he'd made the next day to quit going through women with the same speed he went through underwear. She hadn't been his last one-night stand, but being with her had marked the end of him screwing someone different every night of the week.

High on life and down on himself for the attraction he had to one of his male coworkers at the time, he'd slept his way through half the female population of the county. All the while, trying to convince himself he wasn't gay, that a female could get him off just as easily as his late-night jerk off fantasies, all of which featured tight male bodies and even tighter male asses.

Needless to say, it hadn't worked. And now here he was, in love, and thanks to his randy youth, about to fuck things up for himself royally. He would have to tell Andrew he'd slept with his sister. Wouldn't he?

Then again, as he stood staring down at the picture in his hands, he remembered that Angela was gone, long dead, and couldn't tattle on him. If he didn't confess, Andrew need never know. Right? Things could continue as they were and no one would be the wiser. Keeping silent meant he wouldn't have to worry about risking Andrew's affection.

He couldn't abide lying most of the time, didn't see the point in it, but this seemed like the one exception to the rule. The truth would only hurt everyone involved. There was no telling what Andrew would think or do if he knew about Ryan's impulsive night with his sister. And Ryan simply wasn't willing to chance it. For the first time in his life, he was in love; he wasn't about to open his yap and fuck it up.

Ryan walked out of the house and into the bright afternoon sun, his mind made up about keeping quiet, and headed for where Andrew stood admonishing Katie for throwing the basketball against the house. The stiff way Andrew stood, his back ramrod straight and his chin tilted up, screamed of his aggravation more than the gentle scolding he was in the middle of delivering.

Ryan stood a little off to the side, not listening to the words so much as watching father and daughter interact. Once again, he noticed the differences between the pair. The mismatched build and coloring. Katie really didn't take after Andrew and Angela. Not in the slightest bit.

Katie's shoulders slumped. He saw her bite into her bottom lip, sucking the entire thing into her mouth until only her teeth cutting into the tan skin beneath was visible. An inkling of something gnawed at him. *Remembrance? Recognition?* Whatever it was, it flashed in and out of his mind so quickly he couldn't quite latch onto it.

Then it hit him. Lisa used to do that very thing when she was a kid. Their dad had picked on her, telling her that her lips would stay that way if she kept doing it. The same mannerism Katie had, Lisa had.

His mind spun. Small details began to mount and add up. Andrew had said he didn't know who Katie's father was. That she could have been the result of a one-night stand. Then there was her coloring, the dark hair and not-so-prevalent whiskey-colored eyes, her propensity for art. *Did that mean...? Could she possibly be...?*

Katie was nine. He had no idea when her birthday was, but even without it, the timing was too damn close for comfort.

He spun around, his thoughts chaotic and full of turmoil. Distantly, he heard someone call his name, but he couldn't stop. He had to get out. Had to leave. Now.

A little over an hour later, after finally being able to run off the last of his guests and having talked Jake into letting Katie stay the night with Shawn, Andrew was able to make his way over to Ryan's apartment. Ryan running off the way he had, his face pale and drawn, had Andrew's insides twisted in a knot. No matter the problem, or how scared he was of finding out what had happened, he knew he wouldn't be able to let go of his concern until he found out what was going on.

He approached Ryan's door with the same dread with which someone would cross a minefield. On the other side, Ryan waited with the answer to his questions.

He raised his hand to knock, but the door swung inward before he had the chance to beat on it. Ryan stood in the partially open doorway, a pair of track shorts slung low on his hips. His eyes were bloodshot and a clear bottle of vodka was clutched in one fist. His free hand clenched the door's lip and inched it open a tad more. "Come on in. I've been watchin' for ya. Knew you were bound to show up sooner or later."

Andrew stepped around Ryan, the strong stench of liquor invading his nostrils, and entered the apartment. He heard the door close behind him and turned to see Ryan tipping back the liquor.

"What's with the vodka, Ryan? I thought you said you didn't drink."

"I don't." Ryan stumbled past him and flopped onto the couch.

209

"Then what's with the liquor? The last I checked, no one's yet invented non-alcoholic vodka."

Ryan waved his bottle at the couch beside him. "Sit down, Drew."

Hearing Ryan's nickname for him, the one he usually only used when they made love, had Andrew taking a seat. He perched on the very end of the couch and propped his elbows on his knees.

"What's going on, Ryan?"

Ryan stared at him for a moment, the lines of his face grim. "What's Katie's birthday?"

"Huh?"

"When's Katie's birthday?"

"September twenty-ninth. Listen, I don't know what Katie has to do with this, but..."

Ryan closed his eyes and seemed to concentrate on something. One hand ticked off numbers as if he were adding math in his head.

His behavior was just weird.

Ryan's hands clenched. The one not wrapped around the bottle balled into a fist. His eyes popped open and zeroed in on him. "Do ya have a picture of her?"

"Why, Ryan? Whatever is going on with you has nothing to do with my daughter."

"Do ya?" Ryan repeated.

"Yeah."

"Get it out."

"Ookaay." Andrew pulled out his wallet and rifled through it, coming up with Katie's school picture from the previous fall.

Ryan held out his hand. "Let me see it."

Andrew handed him the picture. Ryan studied it as if the photo held the answers to the mysteries of life.

"What's this about? I thought things were going fine. Or I did, until you took off like you were being chased out."

Ryan handed Andrew back the picture, Katie's cherubic face pointing in Andrew's direction. "Look at the photo, Drew. What do you see?"

"I see Katie, my daughter. What are you trying—?"

"Wrong," Ryan bellowed. "You see *my* daughter."

Huh? It was a good thing Ryan wasn't a big drinker, because he certainly wasn't making any sense at the moment. "Ryan," Andrew said, not even trying to mask his exasperation, "it's obvious you're upset about something, so I'm trying to be patient, but I'd really like to know what the hell you're talking about."

"Here." Ryan pushed the liquor bottle at him. "You're gonna need this."

He took the bottle and set it on the end table beside him. Ryan was talking in riddles and obviously didn't need any more. "I'm not drinking. I think you've drunk enough for the both of us. Now, what the hell's going on? And what does it have to do with Katie?"

Ryan slumped back against the sofa and stared at him, his eyes full of something Andrew didn't want to think of as grief. "Do you 'member how you told me you didn't know who Katie's father was? How she was probably the result of a one-nighter?"

"Yeah, Ryan, I remember, but I don't see what that has to do with—"

"Just shut up and let me 'splain. 'M getting there."

"All right, but get to the point."

"Did I ever tell you 'bout when I was younger? How I didn't

211

wanna be gay, so I forced myself to sleep with a bunch of women to prove to myself that I didn't 'ave to be, unless I wanted to?"

"No."

"Well, I did. And when I was back in your bedroom after you went outside, I saw a picture of one of 'em on the dresser. I slept with your sister and now I'm pretty sure Katie could be mine. How's that for a small world, eh?" Ryan buried his face in his hands and laughed hysterically. The laughter quickly turned to hiccups and finally ended in great wracking sobs that shook his broad frame.

Andrew sat on the couch, his body almost as frozen as his mind. He wanted to console Ryan. He really did, but he couldn't move.

A million little details zipped through his mind. Things Katie said or did. Tiny idiosyncrasies and physical attributes, they all squashed together in the forefront of his numb brain and made it damn near impossible for him to refute Ryan's claim.

There was no reason for Ryan to lie. He had nothing to gain by claiming to be Katie's biological father. And if Ryan was her true father, what did that make Andrew? If a blood test proved Ryan right and Katie was his, would he want custody? Take Katie away from him?

Misty eyes focused on the window behind Ryan, not really seeing it but remembering the view from other times. Life went on all around, while his world was reduced to a pile of ash the slightest wind could blow away at any minute.

Chapter Eight

His head swimming and his eyes a blurred mess, Ryan looked up to see a lone tear cascading down Andrew's cheek. That, more than the silence, more than the agony he felt for hurting the man who meant so much to him, was his undoing.

He scooted over to where Andrew sat and pulled his lover into his arms. Andrew stiffened, but didn't pull away. Ryan hugged him, content to be the only one holding on. He didn't expect any more.

Ryan rested his chin on Andrew's shoulder and whispered, "I'm sorry."

A tremor shook Andrew's slim body. He exhaled a ragged sigh. "What are you going to do?"

"I...I have to know. I'm sorry, but I want a DNA test done. If she is mine..." Ryan couldn't finish his sentence. He didn't know what would happen exactly, if Katie was his daughter.

He wanted to reassure Andrew that he wasn't going to take Katie away from him. If it turned out Katie really was his flesh and blood, he knew he wanted a relationship with her, wanted to be there for her and provide for her, but he wasn't sure about anything more than that. He didn't know if he was cut out to be a single parent or if he would be any good at it.

The little girl clearly loved Andrew, and he her. Wouldn't it be cruel to take her away from the only father she'd ever known? Ryan knew that no matter how hard he tried, he wouldn't make half the parent Andrew did. Maybe they could work something out, arrange visitations or something like divorced parents did?

Everything felt out of joint. So many decisions hung in the balance, waiting for someone to make a choice that would irrevocably change all their lives. It was all so damn confusing and sudden. He wasn't sure what would happen and that in itself was terrifying. Just when Ryan realized he'd fallen in love, he was going to lose Andrew. He hadn't even had the chance to tell Andrew how he'd felt, and now it was too late. It didn't matter. After all this, Ryan was sure Andrew wouldn't want him. He was the one throwing Andrew's life into upheaval, ruining his happy home.

A sharp pain tore through Ryan's chest. His nose burned and his eyes watered. He tightened his arms around Andrew, afraid that if he released him Andrew would walk out on him and refuse to look back. Petrified of losing him, Ryan held on tight, his arms banding like steel around Andrew.

"Let go," Andrew said, his voice hoarse.

"No."

Andrew shoved against his chest. "Let. Me. Go."

Ryan loosened his hold but refused to budge from where he sat. Andrew glared at him with sad, red-rimmed eyes. "Move."

"No."

Andrew shoved against Ryan's shoulders, pushing with all his might, and Ryan knew he meant business. Ryan moved back a few inches, barely creating enough room for Andrew to slide by and unsteadily rise to his feet.

Ryan realized he couldn't force Andrew to stay, even if it killed him to watch him walk away. That didn't, however, mean he had to make it easy on him. "Stay," he pleaded.

Halfway to the door, with his back to Ryan, Andrew stopped.

Taking that as a positive sign, Ryan continued. "Please. Don't go."

"Why? Give me one good reason I should stay."

"I need..."

Andrew spun around and snapped out, "You need what?"

On trembling legs, Ryan crossed the room. "You," he replied softly, his fingertips brushing lightly over Andrew's stubbled jaw. "I need you, Drew."

Andrew's face turned, his mouth a millimeter away from Ryan's fingertips, presenting a lure he couldn't resist. Azure blue eyes met his as he ran the pad of his thumb over Andrew's bottom lip.

Ryan leaned in and kissed Andrew, well aware he was making a mistake. Now was not the time for sex. Yet he couldn't stop himself once he was moving. He kissed Andrew with all the emotion, all the love he felt deep inside. Andrew's flesh remained lax and unresponsive.

Ryan prayed to every deity he'd ever heard of for Andrew to kiss him back, to give him something. Any kind of response to show he wanted this as much as Ryan did. Though he knew he didn't deserve it, all he asked was to have this one night, this one last moment with the man he loved before he was left alone and brokenhearted.

Andrew owned Ryan's heart, his very soul, but there was one thing Ryan could give him that he'd shared with no one else. Through numerous trysts and easy lovers, Ryan had never bottomed. Always a staunch top, the barrier of his anus had yet to be breached by anything larger than a finger. Somehow, he'd always known that his heart and his ass were a package deal. Until Andrew, Ryan had never trusted anyone enough to let

215

them inside. If this was going to be their last night together, he longed to feel Andrew moving inside him, laying claim to a deeper part of him. Ryan could only hope Andrew would take the sacrifice of his cherry for what it was. A gift of trust, the only thing he had left to offer the man he loved.

Tentatively, Ryan slipped his arms under Andrew's. His palms gravitated to Andrew's shoulder blades and settled there, kneading the firm, tense muscles.

Andrew wasn't resisting his touch, but neither was he participating. That wouldn't do at all. Ryan wanted Andrew to take *him*, not the other way around.

"Please," he whispered, his tongue flickering out to tease the corners of Andrew's sealed lips. "Need you, Drew. Need you so damn bad."

A nervous minute passed with no response. He sighed against Andrew's lips, resigned to the fact that he wasn't going to respond. His arms fell to his sides and he took a step back. To his surprise, Andrew grabbed him by the shoulders and pulled him into his arms. Ryan gasped and Andrew's lips converged on his, his tongue slinking past his teeth and swirling around his own. Ryan buried the fingers of one hand in the silky hair at the nape of Andrew's neck, while the other worked on the buttons of Andrew's shirt.

Without stopping to breathe or look where they were going, Ryan began to slowly work his way back to his bedroom. Clothing fell to the wayside, littering the hallway in their wake.

Andrew stopped at the foot of his bed. He kicked out of his shoes and toed his pant legs over his feet. Ryan admired the smooth creamy landscape of Andrew's skin, the rise and fall of his muscled chest. His gaze trailed over the slim tapering of hair beneath Andrew's bellybutton to the thick jut of his cock. The deep rose-colored head was swollen and glistening with excitement. His balls were drawn, cupping the hard base of his stalk.

Ryan's mouth watered and his knees shook. He wanted Andrew to make love to him, was determined for it to happen, but inside he was nervous. Anything new came with a bit of trepidation and he knew the first time was bound to be uncomfortable.

He sat on the foot of the bed and opened his arms to Andrew, who walked right into them and picked up where they'd left off. Ryan eased back onto the mattress. Andrew followed him down, his lips in constant motion.

Ryan groaned and arched into Andrew's touch as his lover pulled and twisted his nipples. The taut peaks stiffened and began to tingle from the attention they were receiving. Andrew's lips left his and a second later the wet heat of his mouth surrounded one of Ryan's nipples, laving and nibbling, while his fingers tortured the other taut nub with short squeezes. Andrew leaned across him, switching sides, and cool air washed over his moistened flesh, making embers of fire bungee to his cock. Fresh blood pumped anew, engorging him to the point of pain. His dick bounced against his stomach, nearly reaching his navel as it strained for attention like an eager puppy.

He reached down to stroke himself, only to have Andrew growl, "Mine," and bat his hand away from his cock.

The low, vicious rumble affected him like a blast of electricity. Ryan's hips rocked up, shoving his groin skyward, searching for...something. Andrew answered his silent plea by scooting down his body and licking at the dripping head of his cock. The hot, wet abrasions against the tight, sensitive skin of his helmet made him whimper, actually fucking whimper, and fist the cover on either side of his hips to keep from pumping upward.

Up and down, around and around, Andrew laved him like a Popsicle. One of Ryan's hands released the cover and ran over the top of Andrew's head, through his hair, anywhere he could reach, encouraging him on. Odd grunts spilled from his mouth, filling the air with a hunger not to be denied.

Andrew flicked his tongue down Ryan's shaft, nibbling at the base, before moving on to mouth the tightly drawn sac protecting his balls. His lips pulled and tugged at it, exerting gentle pressure and loosening the taut skin. Using two fingers, Andrew separated Ryan's balls and laved the hidden base of his cock where it extended down into his body.

Ryan jerked his hips, unable to control his reaction, and pressed himself harder against Andrew's marauding tongue. Ryan moaned and thrashed as Andrew's tongue slipped down and swiped over his pelvic floor and quickly ringed the puckered entrance to his ass.

Andrew rose up and moved between Ryan's splayed thighs. He grabbed a pillow and wedged it underneath Ryan's hips, propping him up. Ryan tensed and clenched his bottom, watching Andrew through heavy lashes as Drew dropped to his belly and squirmed into position between his thighs.

The first hot touch of Andrew's tongue on his anus sent Ryan into a frenzy. He groaned and writhed, pleaded and begged, while Andrew went at him as if he were a starving man facing a gourmet banquet. When he felt the stiff tip of Andrew's tongue breach his entrance, he thought his cock would break from the amount of blood rushing into it, stretching it out past its usual girth.

Andrew rose up on his knees between Ryan's legs and ran the bulbous head of his cock through the slick valley between Ryan's cheeks. Slight pressure against his anus warned Ryan of Andrew's intent to penetrate him. Though slick and loosened from Andrew rimming him, Ryan knew that sex without lube would hurt more than it had to.

He gripped Andrew's forearms, preventing him from pressing in. "Wait, Drew. I've never..." His voice trailed off on a groan as Andrew's cock brushed over his hole. "I've never done this. We need lube. A lot of lube."

"Get it," Andrew grunted.

Ryan scrambled onto his side and reached into the nightstand. He fumbled through crap he couldn't see until his fingers latched onto the smooth cool bottle of lube. Turning back to Andrew, he held it out to him.

Andrew took the bottle and squeezed a huge dollop into his palm. As he worked it over the ruddy length of his prick, his gaze never strayed from Ryan's face. Seeing the potent storm raging in Andrew's blue eyes, Ryan shivered in anticipation.

Andrew milked another glob of lube out of the bottle. His fingers spread the cheeks of Ryan's ass and found the moist entrance into his body. Pressing a finger home, he met Ryan's eyes. "I'm going to fuck you so hard."

Ryan trembled at the slight burn of Andrew's thick finger entering him and the sensual promise in Andrew's voice. "Do it, fuck me."

Andrew's finger retracted, only to push back in with a second. His fingers speared deep, twisting and spreading Ryan open. The tip of one brushed his prostate and caused him to jolt from the extreme pleasure of it. Ryan lifted his legs and gripped them beneath the knees, holding himself open for Andrew. "Please, Drew. Now. Want you inside me."

Andrew grabbed the base of his cock and pressed the wide head to Ryan's entrance. Ryan held his breath, trying to concentrate on loosening his muscles. The fat head of Andrew's cock popped through the restrictive ring of Ryan's ass, causing a lance of sharp, sweet pain. He cried out, unable to hold it in, as Andrew forged deeper, filling him to bursting.

Seated all the way inside, Andrew stilled. His eyes fell shut and his breath burst from his chest in choppy puffs. He'd never looked more beautiful.

His eyes opened and met Ryan's, the connection between them stronger than ever. He leaned down and kissed Ryan, his tongue spearing into Ryan's mouth as his hips began to rock.

On and on, Andrew plunged deeper, tongue and cock working in an alternating rhythm that pitched all conscious thought from Ryan's head. All he knew or experienced was Andrew and what he was doing to his body, the ride he was taking him on. Ryan didn't think he could go higher, feel more, until Andrew reached between their damp, sweat-slick bodies and took hold of his cock. One squeeze and he was shaking, coming so hard his spine felt it had all but dissolved under the pressure. The orgasm shot through his body in flash-lightning intensity and splashed against the feverish skin of his abdomen. "Oh God. Oh shit. Drew!"

Howling, Andrew plunged deep, his hips grinding against Ryan as he found his release. Ryan felt the hot wet spray of Andrew's come inside him and belatedly realized they hadn't used protection. Though he knew it was stupid and irresponsible, he was glad.

Andrew's softening member slid from his body, leaving behind the bitter sting of overstretched muscles. He rolled off of him and collapsed, his arm haphazardly thrown across Ryan's chest. The need to rise and clean himself up was tempting, but Ryan didn't want to move. He rolled to his side and pulled Andrew's arm tight around him. He buried his face in the pillow, his eyes welling with tears he refused to shed.

As Andrew's breath evened out behind him, assuring Ryan

he was sound asleep, he muttered the three words he knew Andrew would no longer want to hear from him. "I love you."

Chapter Nine

Red light pervaded Andrew's closed eyelids and yanked him from the warm embrace of slumber. With reluctance, he slowly stretched like a cat. Extended above his head, his fingertips encountered a wall instead of his headboard, causing his eyes to pop open in confusion.

For a moment, the simplicity of stark white walls didn't register. He rubbed at his gritty eyes and pulled himself upright, blinking groggily.

Ryan's bedroom. Right.

The night before came back to him in bits and pieces. Ryan admitting he'd slept with Angie, Ryan's possible paternity of Katie, fucking Ryan into the mattress. *God.* What the hell had he been thinking? He should have gone home, not stayed and taken the man's cherry.

And just what had that been about? If Ryan had never bottomed before, why had he been so anxious to the night before?

His cock twitched, filling and lengthening as he remembered the sexy way Ryan's body had clung to his. So hot and tight. One hand slipped under the cover to caress his aching flesh.

The tasty smell of frying bacon wafted under his nose. Andrew's stomach growled and overrode his desire to rub one off before leaving the warm bed. He threw his legs over the side and stood, shivering as his feet made contact with the cold hardwood floor.

At the end of the bed, he found his pants and shoes in a discarded heap. He kicked into his Dockers and yanked them up. Working the buttons, he padded down the hall in search of Ryan and sustenance.

Ryan's voice reached him halfway down the hallway. "Yes, tomorrow morning would be fine."

Pause.

"No. Just two of us."

Pause.

"Well, um, the mother is deceased. Would a relative, like a sibling, do?"

Pause.

"Yes. Thank you. We'll see you in the morning at ten."

Ryan was just setting the white cordless phone back on its base as Andrew entered the kitchen. "Who was that?"

Ryan glanced over at him and then returned his attention to the stove, using a fork to turn the bacon, which was snapping and hissing in the frying pan. "Um, well, that was Labcorp. I called to make us an appointment for paternity testing. They can see us in the morning. I hope ten o'clock is good for you and Katie."

Andrew ran a hand through his mangled hair and wondered what he was supposed to say. He felt like he was caught in the middle of a bad soap opera. If it were, he could see the title of today's episode: "Gay lover's secret baby revealed".

The beginnings of a headache thumped at his temples. He absently used his pointer finger to rub at one, while watching

Ryan shimmy around the kitchen fixing breakfast. Normally, the domestic scene would have comforted him. This morning it seemed odd.

"I'm just gonna go get dressed," he mumbled as he walked out of the room.

The hallway walls felt too small and narrow, like they were closing in on him, trying to trap him in. He felt like he should be doing something, saying something, but he didn't know what it was. Throwing a temper tantrum sounded good, maybe even having a bender like Ryan had pulled the night before, but he was an adult and had things to do. Life went on, even when your insides were twisted and bleeding.

He needed to pick Katie up from Jake's and clean the house. The leftover mess from the barbecue still needed to be cleaned up. He'd been in too big a hurry to see about Ryan to deal with it before he'd left.

He and Ryan needed to talk, needed to try and figure out where they went from here, but he was too tired to broach the subject. For the rest of the day, he didn't want to think about it. Tomorrow morning, when they went for testing, would be soon enough.

Andrew pulled on his shirt and stomped into his shoes. His underwear he stuffed into his pocket on the way to the door. Opening it, he turned back to see Ryan standing in the kitchen, watching him, a confused frown on his face.

"You're leaving? I thought maybe we could talk over breakfast."

"Sorry. I have to go. I, uh, I have to pick up Katie."

"Oh. Well, okay. Do you want to meet me in the morning, or would you like for me to come and pick you two up?"

Andrew wanted to say he'd never agreed to the damn test in the first place. Instead, he said, "We'll meet you." And with that, he walked out the door, closing it with a soft click behind him.

Jake yanked open the door and flew out onto the porch before Andrew had finished climbing the stairs. He was dressed in a pair of threadbare jogging pants and nothing more, his hair a tangled riot of curls around his thin face. "Jesus, man, where've you been all day? I called Ryan this morning looking for you, and he said you'd already left. That was over five hours ago. I was about to start calling the hospitals."

"Sorry," Andrew apologized, humbled that he'd found such a good friend in Jake. "I spent most of the morning and afternoon just driving around. Thinking about things."

Actually what he'd done was drive to the park and sit in his car. Half the time he'd stared off into outer space, his mind too chaotic to think straight. The rest of the time, he'd stared at the kids and their parents, trying to picture him and Ryan there with Katie, as a family. And then he'd lectured himself on the foolishness of dreaming.

Going home had sounded good, in theory, but he couldn't stop thinking about how empty the house was without Katie in it, and he hadn't been ready to face the world yet. He paused and shook his head. "Where are the kids?"

"They're in Shawn's room playing video games." Jake grabbed his arm and guided him over to the swing inhabiting one corner of the covered porch. "Tell me what's going on, peanut. It's not like you to up and disappear without telling someone where you're going to be just in case Katie might need you."

"I know. I didn't mean to be gone so long. I guess I phased out there for awhile." Andrew shuddered and sat next to Jake.

Amanda Young

"I found out some..." he paused while he tried to find the right word, "interesting news last night."

"And...?" Jake urged him to continue.

"You know how I've always kinda wondered about who Katie's biological father is?"

"Yeah."

"Well, now I don't have to wonder anymore."

"Andrew." Jake sighed. "You're going to have to do better than that. I have no idea what you're talking about."

"Yesterday, Ryan saw a picture of Angie. The one I keep on my bedroom dresser. He recognized her."

Jake sucked in a sharp breath. "Oh my fucking God. Are you trying to say what I think you are?"

Andrew frowned at the smile on Jake's face. "Why are you smiling? For God's sake, I just told you my lover slept with my sister. He could take Katie away from me. You could be a little sympathetic."

"I don't see what the big deal is, peanut. So what if he banged Angie. Are you saying Ryan thinks he might be..." he looked around them and leaned in closer before continuing, "Katie's father?"

Andrew nodded. Usually he liked Jake's whimsical approach to life, but right now it got on his nerves. What the hell was there to be happy about?

"So, what were you driving around feeling sorry for yourself all day about? What could be better than finding out the man you love is the father of your child? You should be thrilled."

"Yeah, you idiot, I'm really thrilled. What if he tries to take her away? Huh? Did you think of that? It's not every day you find out you may be a father. What if he wants her? I can't lose her, Jake. Katie's all I have. She's my little girl."

226

"You know I love you, so don't take this the wrong way, but don't you think you're being just a little overdramatic about all this? I have a hard time believing that Ryan would want custody of Katie. The man loves you; I can't see him doing that. Did he tell you that's what he'd want?"

"No, but—"

"No buts. Just hear me out first. The two of you love each other—"

Andrew scoffed. "Ryan doesn't—"

"Ack. I said for you to stay quiet and hear me out. And yes, Ryan does love you. It's obvious to everyone but you. Now, as I was saying, you guys are in love. *If* Katie is Ryan's biological daughter, it seems to me that's the icing on the cake. I mean think about it. Angie was your twin. That makes Katie almost yours DNA wise. If you throw Ryan's swimmers into the mix, hell, it's almost like the two of you created her together. Other than a divine miracle, that's the closest you're ever gonna get to having a naturally conceived child with the man you love."

Andrew chewed his bottom lip. He hadn't thought of things that way. "That's all well and good, but for your information, oh wise one, Ryan has never once said he loves me."

"Have you told him how *you* feel?"

"No. So what?"

"Well, does the fact that you haven't told him how you feel mean you don't love him?"

"I never said I loved him." Even to his own ears, he was beginning to sound like a recalcitrant child. That certainly wasn't good, but damn, he didn't want to agree with Jake. He'd wanted someone to bemoan to, not someone to jump on the happily-ever-after wagon.

"But you do," Jake replied cockily.

"Whatever, Jake. Would you go in and fetch Katie for me? I need to take her home." What he didn't say was that he needed to get himself home more. Between his own walls, he would be able to mope and lick his wounds in peace. He could spend time with Katie and try to figure out how to explain why they were going to the doctor. He definitely wasn't ready to tell her the truth.

Chapter Ten

Dawn crested the horizon and splattered watery light over Ryan's prone body. He slapped the pillow in aggravation and sat up. Enough was enough. Since Andrew had walked out on him the previous morning, he hadn't been able to do anything; not eat or sleep. The breakfast he'd been in the process of cooking yesterday morning was promptly flung into the trash bin. Watching Andrew walk away without a single glance back had killed something inside Ryan.

The only thing he'd managed to accomplish since then was thinking, about anything and everything under the sun. The pros and cons had been weighed and reweighed a dozen or more times. He knew what he wanted. All he had to do was convince Andrew.

Ryan slipped from bed and hurried to the closet. He pulled on the first thing his fingers touched, jeans and a black T-shirt. Now that his mind was made up, he was in too big a hurry to search for his shoes. He slipped on a pair of ugly green flip-flops lying at the foot of the bed, the ones he used when he wanted to go out and check the mail, and finger combed his hair on the way to the door.

Halfway out, he remembered his keys and turned back to grab them off the hook beside the door. He wouldn't get far without those.

Jangling keys in hand, he jogged across the pavement to his bike. Straddling it, he punted the kickstand up. His ass hit the leather seat, his fingers twisted the key in the ignition, and he was off.

Wind whipped at his face, tore at his hair and clothing, as he revved the bike up and flew over the road. The chill sting biting into his skin invigorated him, drove his sense of purpose higher. He could do this. He would. Andrew would hear him, return his affection, and they would live happily ever after. No problem.

Yeah right, his subconscious yelled back to him, *you wish.* "Shut up," he whispered, pulling onto Andrew's street. As he closed in on Andrew's house, he slowed the bike and walked it the last block. He didn't want the loud rumble to wake Katie. He didn't know how sound a sleeper she was, and what he needed to tell Andrew had to be said in private.

Which was why he forewent ringing the bell and walked around the side of the house instead. If any of Andrew's neighbors was up and saw him slinking around outside, they would probably think he was a burglar and call the cops, but that was a chance he was willing to take.

Ryan sidled up to Andrew's bedroom window, thanking the stars the man had a first-floor bedroom, and knocked lightly. He couldn't see in because of the blinds, but the house was dark, giving him as good a chance as any of catching him in bed. He hoped Andrew had been able to get more rest than he had, though Ryan doubted it.

When a couple of seconds went by, he knocked again. The blinds rustled, separating, and Andrew's face appeared in the window. His beautiful blue eyes were bloodshot and a thick growth of dark blond stubble marred his jaw. Seeing the way his lover looked, so worn out and miserable, tore at Ryan's heartstrings. He would've sold his left nut to wipe away all the hurt and worry he'd caused him.

Andrew's eyes widened when he saw him. He raised a brow and then the blind fell back over the window. Ryan's heart felt like it'd taken a shot of adrenaline as the seconds passed by. Was Andrew going to ignore him, leave him standing out here with his heart on his sleeve?

He swallowed the ball of dread steadily building in his throat. His eyes misted and he blinked the tears away. His fists flexed and his resolve hardened.

No. He wasn't going to let it be over this quick. The least Andrew could do was hear him out. If he still wanted Ryan to go after that, then he would, but he would have his say first. He raised his hand to knock again.

"Are you going to stand out here and admire my window all morning, or are you going to come in the house?"

Ryan jolted at hearing Andrew's voice. His head turned and he saw Andrew standing at the corner of the house, a ratty blue terrycloth robe hanging off his shoulders. The front was open, exposing the pale creaminess of Andrew's chest and the firm, defined contours of his abdomen. A pair of loose blue sleep pants hung low on his hips, revealing the sweet V of delicate skin between the jut of his hipbones.

In spite of his reasons for being there, his mouth watered for a taste of what he knew was beneath the thin cotton. He felt his dick react to the visual stimulus and had to shake his head to clear out the cobwebs of desire building. If things went they way he wanted—and they would, damn it—he and Andrew would have the rest of their lives to make love.

"Well, are you coming?"

Ryan snapped to attention and crossed the feet separating them. His arms ached to hold Andrew, but he refrained from reaching for him and stuck his hands in his pockets instead. "I had to talk to you."

"It's okay. I was awake. Couldn't sleep last night." Andrew's gaze crawled over his disheveled appearance. "By the looks of you, I'd say you didn't either. You look like shit."

Ryan smiled. It was a small one but it felt good nonetheless. "Thanks a lot. You don't look so hot yourself, Drew."

"Yeah, well, there's a good reason for that. Come on into the house. I want to show you something I found last night. I was just getting ready to call you, when you knocked on the, err, window."

"Okay. There are some things I need to share with you too."

They somberly walked into the house together. Andrew led him into his bedroom and shut the door. "Katie's still asleep. That kid will sleep until noon unless I wake her up."

"Sounds like me," Ryan said and then bit his tongue when he realized his slip. *Damn.* That wasn't the way he wanted to start the conversation.

"That's not surprising, considering what I found when I went through some of the things Angie left behind last night." He walked over to the bed and perched on the side. His hand went to the nightstand and rested on the drawer's knob. With his other hand, he patted the bed. "Come over and sit with me. There's something I want to show you."

Though he had a strong curiosity to find out what Andrew was up to, he needed to speak first, to explain what was on his mind before he lost his nerve. "It can wait for a minute, Drew. We need to talk."

With the drawer halfway open, Andrew's hand froze. "But I know—"

"Please. I need you to hear me out."

"All right. Go ahead and say whatever it is you need to."

"Thank you." Ryan sat beside Andrew and pulled one of his hands into his. Now all he had to do was tell Andrew how he felt and remember to breathe. That should be easy, right? "I did a lot of thinking last night. Actually, that's pretty much all I did after you left. Anyway, here's the thing."

Ryan swallowed. "I'm sorry that I slept with Angie. If I could take it back, I would in a heartbeat. I would do anything to make you happy. I love you. I mean, I *really* fucking love you and the thought of losing you terrifies me. So, if you don't want to go through with the paternity test, I'll cancel it. It isn't important anyway. Whether or not Katie is my flesh and blood doesn't matter because I'm going to be around to help you parent her anyhow, right? Regardless of her DNA, I would love her anyway because she's a part of you."

Ryan sucked in a deep breath of air. So much for remembering to breathe. Between his palms, Andrew's hand was cool and dry. He wanted to look up and search Andrew's face for some sign of what he was feeling, but Ryan was scared to. He'd never been afraid of anything in his life, but damned if he wasn't quaking in terror now. His entire life hung in the balance, waiting to hear what Andrew would say.

He felt a hand on his shoulder and looked up more out of reflex than intent. Andrew had scooted closer and was right beside him, a Mona Lisa smile on his face and his big blue eyes luminous with unshed tears. "You big idiot."

That wasn't exactly the "I love you" Ryan was hoping to hear but the kiss Andrew leaned in and pressed against his closed mouth more than made up for the slight. Ryan wrapped his arms around Andrew, pulled him in for a tight hug and buried his face in Andrew's neck. The feel of Andrew's body next to him, the smell of his lover's skin and hair, comforted Ryan like nothing else could have.

Andrew kissed the curve of Ryan's neck. "I love you too. So, so much, Ryan. Too much to try and keep you from finding out whether or not Katie's yours. If you would have let me finish telling you what I found out last night, you would already know she's your daughter."

Ryan pulled back, not by much though, only enough so that he could see Andrew's face. "What? But how?"

Katie was his daughter. His. He didn't know what he should have been feeling, apprehension, maybe even anger at being kept in the dark for so long, but all he felt was happiness. Andrew was in love with him and he'd just found out he was a father. It was a bit much to absorb.

Andrew brushed his lips softly over Ryan's and turned to pull a yellowed envelope out of his nightstand. "After Katie went to bed last night, I went through some of Angie's things again. There isn't much, just some trinkets and jewelry mostly, but inside the lining of her jewelry case was a letter addressed to Katie. I don't know why I never noticed it before, but then again I hadn't ever looked for something before either." He held out the letter. "Here. You read it."

Ryan took the envelope and gently removed a piece of pink stationery embossed with white daisies along one side. The handwriting upon it was in large and painstakingly neat cursive.

My Dearest Katie,

If you're reading this, then I have to assume I've passed away and left you in the care of your uncle Andrew. I'm so sorry I wasn't able to stay with you and watch you grow up to become the wonderful young woman I have no doubt you've become.

Nevertheless, I know Andrew has raised you well and with

all the love I myself would have bestowed upon you, had I been able to stay. I love you, sweetheart, and I'm sure that whatever you've chosen to do with your life, you would have made me proud.

Since this letter was tucked away inside my jewelry box, I feel confident that you're of an appropriate age to take care of the bobbles I left behind for you and that you're finally old enough to learn the truth of your conception. It isn't a pretty fairy tale for children, but the story of a woman desperate for a child. Desperate to have you, my own sweet little angel, before it was too late.

At twenty-six I was diagnosed with breast cancer and terrified that the one dream I held closest to my heart, the dream to someday have a child, would never come to fruition. I can't excuse my actions but I can try to explain them, so that one day you might be able to understand and, hopefully in time, learn to forgive me for denying you the chance to know your father.

The man who sired you is named Ryan Ward. At the time of your conception, he was a college student at Virginia Tech. I'm sorry, but that's all I can tell you about him. It's all I know. Your father was a man I met and picked up in a bar. I manipulated him and conceived you, without his knowledge or consent. Your biological father didn't abandon you or not care about your wellbeing. Because of my deceit, he doesn't know of your existence. What I did was a despicable, terrible thing to do, but I have to admit that I wouldn't change a thing, because the end result was worth it. After all, it gave me you.

I hope you can find it in your heart to one day forgive me.

Love,

Mom

Ryan read over the note twice and then again. After the third pass, his hands shook so badly he was forced to hand the

235

paper back to Andrew for fear he would inadvertently crumple it. It was Katie's last memento from her mother and for that reason he refrained from wadding it into a ball and throwing it against the wall.

She had purposefully gotten pregnant and kept his child from him. Granted, they hadn't exactly exchanged contact information, but she could have found him if she'd wanted to. Oddly, he felt more pity toward her than anger. The past couldn't be undone and there was no one left to be angry at.

He watched Andrew tuck the note safely back within its envelope and slip it back into the drawer from which it came. When Andrew rotated back around, Ryan pulled him into his lap and enfolded Andrew in his arms.

"Where do we go from here, Drew? Do we tell Katie the truth now, or wait until she's older and better able to understand?"

Andrew nuzzled the side of his neck. "I'll leave that up to you. If you want her to know now, we'll tell her an edited version and save the rest for when she's ready."

"I think I'd like to wait. At least until we've had time to get used to each other. It might come as less of a shock that way."

Andrew nodded. "I think that's probably for the best, all things considered. For what it's worth, I'm sorry. Angie was a good person. I can't picture her doing something like this, but I'm glad she did. Katie's a great kid." He lifted his head and smiled. "I think she must get that from her father."

Her father. That would take some getting used to.

Ryan smiled back. "Yeah, I think you might be right." As his lips met Andrew's and they tumbled over onto the bed, Ryan was optimistic about the future. If he and Andrew could overcome this hurdle, they could make it through the trials and tribulations ahead. For the want of a child's love, his daughter had been conceived. Through the want of an everlasting love of a man, their family was born.

About the Author

Amanda Young spends her days basking in the sun by the seashore and her nights surrounded by dozens of serenading male strippers whose only desire is to make her happy.

Yeah, right.

In real life, my husband would chase away all the hot men, right before asking me what I'm going to fix him for dinner and reminding me to do the dishes for the umpteenth time.

Always an avid reader of romance, I was thrilled when I discovered erotic romance. For a long while I toyed with the idea of writing my own but could never find the time.

When I found myself unemployed, I decided that it was high time I gave it a shot. I sat down at my trusty computer and, according to my very patient husband, haven't moved since.

To learn more about Amanda Young, please visit www.AmandaYoung.org. Send an email to Amanda Young at AmandasRomance@aol.com.

Look for these titles by *Amanda Young*

Now Available:

Missing in Action

Shameful

Taboo Desires

Sins of the Past

Print Anthology

Temperature's Rising

LaVergne, TN USA
31 May 2010
184489LV00016B/1/P